The Hourglass Pendant
and Other Paul James Mysteries

by Pete Howard

DORRANCE
PUBLISHING CO
EST. 1920
PITTSBURGH, PENNSYLVANIA 15238

Dorrance Publishing Co
585 Alpha Drive
Pittsburgh, PA 15238
Visit our website at www.dorrancebookstore.com

ISBN: 978-1-6386-7230-2
eISBN: 978-1-6386-7583-9

The Hourglass Pendant is a collection of ten interconnected short mysteries narrated by Paul James, an understated detective trying to heal from PTSD after witnessing a school shooting. Hired by a mysterious international agency, he begins a cathartic journey across an American frontier filled with danger, romance, and strangely wonderful characters.

Special thanks to Greg Lay for his excellent artwork, which brings extra life to the stories, and to Nancy Andolina for her support and keen artistic sensibility.

Contents

Illustrations by Greg Lay.

A Dream Collage

I tried writing down some of the dreams as I awoke from them. For the most part, it was like blindly chasing after some quick thing that had anticipated my pursuit. By the time I had pen in hand, most of the visions had receded to the margins of memory, like the last rippling from a stone tossed into a pond. Nonetheless, I was able to capture some of the images and occurrences in my attempt to explain the powerfully real emotions elicited by the dreams, some of them weird and disturbing, others indescribably beautiful.

I am startled by a single clap of thunder, followed by silence—a flock of birds takes flight over a roiling, blood-red sea.

A dark corridor leads me toward a dim light. I enter the empty room of an old schoolhouse. The blackboard fades away, becomes a window that looks over an open field. I fly across the green space, joyous, for a moment knowing the ineffable serenity of the afterlife.

A glass globe hovers before me. I cup it in my hands. It is cold, yet vibrates with life, and as I let go, it floats into a rainbow sky.

High on a rocky cliff, two giant statues of angels lean over a churning ocean. A man with wings stands between them, unstable in the heavy, grey air.

A tall figure clad in animal skins approaches me from a forest, whispering in a tongue I cannot understand. We are at the edge of a lake, where she holds a lantern shaped like an hourglass.

I sit high above the earth in the chair of an amusement ride at night, alone among stars. Below, in the dawning light, a swan-white ship sails on the amber sea.

On the ground at my feet the body of a large man lies motionless. Suddenly he turns to me. He has no eyes, and as I kick at him he disappears.

There is a woman, so beautiful, always changing colors and forms. So elusive. So strange, yet so familiar. I know now that she is what love is.

It was in the resurfacing from the depth of such dreams that I heard the knock at the door of my room at the halfway house. It was my parole officer, who had in his hand the papers that signified the end of my debt to society. With hardly a word, he was gone, and I was left there sitting on my cot surrounded by four dim walls, trying to imagine how I would proceed in the real world, the weight of which had all but buried my soul.

I used to be a cop, a good one. I rose through the ranks quickly to sergeant, and I was assigned some of the department's most difficult cases. A few years ago, I was called to an emergency at an elementary school. I arrived at the same time the shooter turned his gun on himself, moments after he had rained hundreds of bullets from his automatic weapon on a classroom of third-grade students. I found them on the floor amid shallow pools of blood. Several who had escaped the bullets were sobbing from beneath their desks.

Six months later I got word that a seven-year-old girl had gone missing after school, and that a pedophile I had collared years ago had recently violated his parole. He was a huge and dull witted-man and had been spotted near his old haunt—the projects surrounding the school. I arrived just before dark. It had snowed that day, and I saw the large footprints behind the school leading toward an alley. I followed, running now, through a half mile of the twisting streets and alleyways. Then I saw him, hunkering over the petrified girl beneath a fire escape. When he saw me, he left the girl and started running. I shot and hit him in the shoulder, but he kept going.

Then, startled by the sudden flurry of pigeons near a dumpster, he tripped and fell. In a fit of rage, I began kicking him, yet this seemed to have little effect on his huge frame. As he turned to face me, I shot him in the groin. Then I shot him again and again and again as he yelled for mercy.

Somehow the brute survived, and he is now serving a life sentence in prison. As for me, I was tried and convicted in civil court for using excessive force. A mostly sympathetic jury and judge sentenced me to minimum-security prison for six months. Yet the authorities made it clear to me that I should never touch a gun again in my life, and that my career as a policeman was over.

It was during my idle time in prison, and later at the halfway house, that the affliction of dreams took root. I attempted to fill the void through various activities. I mastered Sudoku and learned to play jazz guitar. I read a hundred books and even tried to write one; but without an occupation—a real purpose of some sort—my mind could not quiet itself. I tried different forms of antidepressants, but soon the dreams became immune to them. Even during the waking hours, the visions imposed themselves upon me, causing me to question my own sanity. This was my state of mind on the day of my release.

As I stood by the bed packing my suitcase and preparing to re-enter society, I heard a knock at my door. A small, dark-skinned man in a green and gold uniform stood there, no higher than the doorknob. At first I thought I was imagining him, but then he spoke in a high-pitched voice. "Are you Mr. Paul James?" he asked.

The little man handed me an envelope. "Please read this. It is an opportunity for you to consider. I will return in one hour."

Dear Mr. James,

We are aware of what you have gone through recently, and we wish you the best as you recover from those terrible events that brought you here. We are also aware that you will be needing employment as you re-enter society.

What we can offer through our private enterprise is the opportunity for you to resume work as an investigator. We understand that you are prohibited from carrying a gun. This is not of concern to us, as the nature of most of our cases rarely involves such violence. However, this is not to say that your assignments would be without some degree of peril.

The specific terms of employment are detailed in the attached form, which is to be returned through our messenger, Agent Smith. We are certain you will appreciate the generosity of our offer in terms of salary and accommodations. We are also confident that you will welcome the challenging nature of the cases as well as the travel involved. Perhaps such adventure could serve to displace those visions that have plagued you.

We hope you will accept our offer and sign the papers when Agent Smith returns. Should you accept, there is one unpleasant requirement: Agent Smith will implant a chip in your buttocks. This is not to spy on you, but rather to be able to locate you in a time of great need. You will also be issued a phone dedicated to your receiving instructions or information from us.

Again, Mr. James, let us reassure you that this offer is designed to be mutually beneficial. We have great confidence in your investigative instincts and your integrity.

Sincerely,
The Tower

How could they know this about me? I had confided in so few people throughout my ordeals. I began to wonder if this was just another one of my hallucinations. But an hour later, there was knock at the door. Agent Smith had returned.

I accepted the job. You see, I am a loner by nature, with no surviving immediate family or meaningful personal relationships. And I had no place to live at the time. This would be a second chance in life for me, and I seized it, despite knowing absolutely nothing about this agency that refers to itself as *The Tower.* I have never been privy to the inner workings of *The Tower.* I have no knowledge of its infrastructures, its national or corporate affiliations, or even its agendas, which I can only assume are humane and environmentally concerned, based on the nature of my assignments. All I know for sure is that I have been well protected and rewarded on this journey leading to people and places I could scarcely have imagined.

The Hourglass Pendant

I

It began with small animals—rabbits, squirrels, a string of stray cats, and a couple of small dogs that had wandered from home. The Phillipsberg Psychiatric Center employees who found the bodies near the woods at the edge of the hospital lawn assumed it was the work of a large predator—a coyote, cougar, maybe even a rabid coon. But there was the nagging question: why would the victims be left there in the open, with little blood at the scene? It became clear this was the work of a human, maybe a sadistic teenager, or someone performing an obligatory initiation rite for a local gang. After a woman was found dead with a needle stuck in her neck, the Phillipsberg City Police Department launched an intensive investigation.

My directive came via a text message from *The Tower* two weeks after the murder of the middle-aged woman—Peggy Johnson, a direct care aide at the hospital. The local police had uncovered little in their investigation, and they had yet to determine any suspects or motive. There was no explanation as to why she was out there at night alone, and they could only assume that her attacker was hiding in that small patch of woods along the bike path connecting the hospital to the city park. She died of chemical poisoning through a drug overdose. According to the local crime lab, the injected drug was some crudely produced cocktail of oxycodone and Novocain. It was then assumed that the animals had suffered the same death. An autopsy of one of the dogs (disinterred from the owner's yard) confirmed this.

II

It was a hot and muggy August evening with no rain in the forecast when I pulled into the parking lot of the police department in Phillipsberg, North Carolina. Only one officer was present—a tall, African American man who was leaning over a large desk, intensely studying what appeared to be a map or set of blueprints, his finger tracing a pattern across it. He looked up sharply, as he had not heard me enter, and excused himself, hurriedly rolling up the prints.

"You must be Mr. James," he said, extending a long, elegant brown hand toward me and smiling pleasantly despite the perspiration gathering around his brow. "Welcome to summertime in North Carolina! I'm David Thompson, and I've been put in charge of the investigation. We're glad you're here because, to be blunt, we've got nothing on this case. We need a fresh set of eyes, and I've heard that you have excellent vision, so to speak."

After a brief discussion of the state of the investigation, Officer Thompson led me outside the station and pointed to my hotel just down the street along the city park. He informed me that his department would help in any way it could, and that he had arranged for me to meet with some of the staff at the Psychiatric Center the next morning. The hospital was less than a mile from the hotel. He suggested I walk that way in the morning, as it would take me through the woods and across the lawn where the crimes had been committed. He would be in touch with me personally tomorrow afternoon.

I was pleasantly surprised to discover a good restaurant in the hotel. The bar area was clean with soft, multicolored lighting. In the evening, there was a four-piece band that played jazz and blues with great feel, and without being too loud or busy. The waitress was petite, friendly, and very efficient, and the lemon salmon and white wine were both excellent.

From my hotel window I looked north across the park. In the fading light, beyond the wooded area, stood the Phillipsberg Psychiatric Center—a very old, castle-like edifice, its mass of dark stone walls and arched window casings rising to a single spire under the hazy half-moon.

III

The security guard, George Seacrest, greeted me formally as I arrived at the Center the next morning. He led me down a narrow hallway to the office of Dr. Margaret Fredericks, Chief Psychiatrist at the center, who sat at her desk shuffling intently through a pile of folders. As I entered, the Doctor stood to greet me. She was an impressive figure—well over six feet tall in heels, with long, blond hair and wearing a tight fitting silver and black pantsuit. Yet it seemed to me that her puffed lips and full, rounded bosom and buttock were incongruous with her large-boned, angular frame. Heavy facial makeup made it difficult to tell her age.

"Inspector James, welcome." she said, motioning for me to take a seat by her desk. "As you know, these are tough times. The whole city is looking at us like we are the mother of all evil, and to be sure, there is something dreadful going on out there. So how can I assist you in your investigation?"

My first request was for a blueprint of the building, at which she laughed.

"The building is over 150 years old, Mr. James. There is no official blueprint. We have some property maps, appraisals, floor plans, and some sketches from reconstruction companies that have done work here, but that's about it."

She continued assertively. "As you probably already know, the city police have looked extensively at our surveillance tapes, inside and outdoors. They found nothing. We are a high security facility, Mr. James. We monitor everything—the elevators, the stairways, the hallways, all the exits—there is no evidence of someone inside this building having escaped. Whoever did this must have come from somewhere else."

I assured her that I would take all that into consideration, but that I would need to personally review all tapes and maps and floor plans. In addition, I would need a list of the names, job titles, and shifts of all the hospital's over 100 employees. I was determined that, while the city continued their investigation into the neighborhoods surrounding the hospital, I would begin mine from the inside.

It was apparent that the doctor was anxious to get back to her paperwork. "Now, as you can see, I am very busy here. If you will excuse me, Mr. Seacrest will assist you in your efforts here today"

IV

George Seacrest was a 60-year-old Phillipsberg native, one who kept his ears to the ground and eyes all around. He informed me that the murder victim, Peggy Johnson, was a middle-aged LPN who worked a swing shift, and filled in as needed on all floors, especially since recent budget cuts had resulted in employee lay-offs of direct care staff. She was single, quiet, and mostly kept to herself. What she was doing out on that path at night was beyond comprehension—it had been gang contested territory for years.

Seacrest also offered a brief history of the institution. The Psychiatric Center had admitted some of the most dire mental cases in North Carolina's history, including three notorious serial killers. In 1984 a human rights advocacy group filed a lawsuit against the hospital for patient abuse. The case became big news and was sensationalized on Geraldo Rivera's TV show. Consequently, a new set of stringent state regulations was implemented, and along with renewed government funding and political promising, the institution began to grow, admitting more new patients and hiring more people—folks of various professions and all levels of education. It became one of the largest employers in the city.

However, employee turnover was high, largely because the regulations imposed by the state were often prohibitive of sensible and effective behavior management of the patients. There were numerous complaints about the unreasonable restrictions placed on the workers, along with exaggerated reports of bizarre, dangerous, and lunatic incidents. The bars on the weekends were filled with low level employees, present and former, mimicking shamelessly the outlandish behaviors of the clients they cared for.

It was nearly ten o'clock when Head Nurse Gail Henry met me in the lobby. It was her assignment to assist me in my investigation. We began with a tour of the facility.

V

Nurse Henry was a ten-year veteran of the hospital staff and, as I learned later, a widow. Despite her engaging smile and professional manner, I sensed immediately that there was a wall around her, a shield that her black, brooding eyes could not conceal. A hundred warning lights went off in my head, and I forced myself to refrain from trying to penetrate that which was none of my business. Yet it also seemed that she was already aware of what I had perceived.

"Prepare yourself, Mr. James," she said matter-of-factly. "There are secrets here that no one in his right mind would ever want to know about."

Nurse Henry led me down to the end of the hall, through a latched door, then up a series of switch-back staircases all the way to the attic. Our footsteps echoed through the musty hollowness as we entered the sprawling room. It had served as a storage area until recently when it was largely emptied out. Some large items remained—stuffed chairs and couches, tables, cabinets—all hulking in the half-light like large, petrified animals beneath the dusty sheets. The windows overlooking the back lawn had been boarded up after vandals repeatedly bombarded them with rocks. The short door leading to the rusty black iron fire escape was also securely boarded from the inside.

From the attic, we descended to the fourth floor, which was populated by Senior citizens, many of them African American. It was a quiet place, modestly furnished with the barest necessities. Many of the patients were bed-ridden, though some were ambulatory, scuffing in their slippers up and down the hallways. The nurse informed me that these folks experienced various degrees of dementia, yet they really were no different than other seniors who inhabited the privately owned or county operated nursing homes throughout the city. They were here because they could not afford to be elsewhere, and because the state agreed to provide some funding for this purpose.

The third floor housed the most manageable and hopeful patients—the ones who had responded positively to medication and therapy. There were eight rooms along the single hallway, four on either side, with a lounge area in the middle overlooking both north and south lawns of the institution. The windows' exteriors were covered with steel meshing to protect against rocks and to prevent patients from jumping. A middle-aged woman stared out from the south window, rocking back and forth, humming an unfamiliar melody. From one of the rooms I heard a loud male voice laughing hysterically at a TV show.

The second floor was quieter, with younger patients, many who suffered from various forms of addiction, mostly drugs. Others experienced bi-polar symptoms, PTSD, and anxiety disorders. There was hope for some, the nurse said. New, less invasive forms of treatment, including light therapy, had shown some long-term promise. She pointed to one young female, Amanda, who had been a compulsive cutter. It had been two months now since her last incident. The patients on the second floor, in general, had been victims of their home environments and/or traumatic life experiences.

I followed the nurse down the main winding staircase to the first-floor lobby, then through a long corridor leading to a heavy metal door. She unlocked the door, startling a security guard who had been dozing at his desk. We had now entered an annex—a part of the building that was originally used as headquarters, offices, and bunkers for the building architects and managers over a hundred years ago. It had since been remodeled as a ward for the patients diagnosed with the most extreme psychotic disorders, all heavily medicated to reduce the threats they might pose to themselves or others. The ward was eerily quiet as we entered. All the patients were sleeping while a staff member cleaned the floor. The nurse kept our visit there short.

From the annex, we returned to the lobby where another locked door led us down rickety stairs to the basement. This was a single, open room covering the entire space beneath the main building consisting of a complex network of ducts, pipes, cables, valves, and steel posts—the plumbing, electrical wiring, and reinforcement systems that were all part of the building's reconstruction during the 1980's.

On our way back through the lobby, we crossed paths with one of the maintenance workers—a slight, hunch-backed man who carried a broom and dustpan. He seemed in a hurry to get past us. "Oh, Mr. Tomkins," said Nurse Henry, with a playfully antagonistic tone. "Would you like to meet Inspector James? He's here to investigate all kinds of things" Tomkins scowled and skulked away.

"Mr. Tomkins is a bit of a thief." Hands on her hips, she watched him sidle down the hallway. "He takes things from the rooms of the patients, mostly objects given to them from relatives as tokens of concern. I don't know why he hasn't been fired."

My tour of the grounds ended as Office Thompson arrived. With apologies, he informed that no new leads had come to his department.

I spent the evening looking through the documents provided by Dr. Frederick. It seemed her assessment of the building's security was correct. It was clear that that no one could have left the building through any of the doors or windows without having been recorded. Thus, I determined that if anyone from within had found a way out, it would be somewhere under the radar—a place where there is no light yet a path through darkness. Tomorrow I would focus on the first floor annex.

VI

(I confess that as I followed Nurse Henry through the corridor and toward the first-floor ward, I could not help but notice that, despite the traditionally drab, knee-length, loose-fitting white nurse's uniform, there was a very beautiful and robust figure of a woman. I wanted to look directly into her well-deep eyes. And I wanted to believe that she felt something for me as well. I was beginning to feel like I was losing my grip on reality in this house of insanity, and I was desperate for someone I could trust, for anything that might serve to allay the dreams that were stirring...)

We entered the first-floor ward to the smell of strong antiseptics and the sound of TV's turned down low. A cleaning lady had just finished mopping the floor and was stowing her pail and mop in the closet at the end of the hall. Nurse Henry introduced her as Molly, who despite being deaf and dumb was an excellent worker.

Room 101 was occupied by Samuel Baker, a middle-aged man who appeared very normal as he watched the History Channel on his TV. As the nurse introduced us, he rose and shook my hand eagerly. "So nice to meet you sir. Welcome. I hope you enjoy your stay here in London. There are many wonderful sights to see. My wife and I do enjoy traveling."

Nurse Henry informed me that Samuel was having a good week. He was delusional most of the time, often lost in dark and frightful places. Yet lately his mental journeys had been safe and uneventful.

In Room 102, Annie, a petite black woman in a green nightgown, sat silently on the edge of her bed facing the window, rocking back and forth rhythmically, her eyes half closed. She wore an exquisite gold necklace, its pendant a miniature hourglass within a frame that appeared to be carved from jade.

"Hello Annie," said Nurse Henry affectionately. "This is Mr. James. He is a real detective. Can you say hello to him?" Annie did not speak, nor did she look at us. Rather, she continued to gaze out the window, her eyes moving gracefully, peacefully, as if they followed something in flight. All the while she touched her hourglass pendant, turning it gently up, then down, the fine white sand reversing its flow with each turn.

"Annie is a mystery," said Nurse Henry. "She was delivered here by police during a storm on Christmas Eve three years ago. She has no papers, no family, no missing persons reports that match her description, no clues at all as to who she really is." She touched Annie tenderly on her cheek. "Annie is our little orphan."

Petunia Piazza occupied room 103. She was diagnosed as having DID—Dissociative Identity Disorder—three years ago. As the nurse introduced me to her, Petunia blushed and turned away. "Oh, not today," she said. "Papa told me to stay put. I'm not to go out for a while, not until the weather changes."

Nurse Henry informed me that Petunia employs two very separate personalities— "Tunia," the demure girl I just witnessed, and another, "Pat" who is very aggressive, characterized by spitting, cussing, and hurling insults at others.

In room 104, William "Billy" Barnes crouched on the floor behind his bed amid his toys—a GI Joe, a Barbie Doll, a firetruck, and oddly, a Rubik's cube. There were also several bottles of hand sanitizer. Despite his crouching position and child-like demeanor, I could tell Billy was a very large man. He ignored us as he fidgeted with the cube. "Classic case of germaphobia," said the nurse blandly. Billy looked up at her sharply, his face a huge, twisted moon of depravity. But his anger quickly dissolved into a bursting of tears. "I feel sick," he cried in a high-pitched voice . "This place is filthy, and someone needs to clean it."

"He came to us recently, and he is a real pain in the ass, I am sorry to say," said the nurse. As we were leaving, I could hear him cursing, his voice now deep and menacing.

Room 105 belonged to Carlos Benitez, who suffered from schizophrenic delusions. He heard voices, apparently terribly frightening voices. In his extremely agitated states, Nurse Henry informed me, he would hide beneath his bed and scream and/or giggle for days. He was briefly distracted from his present obsession as Nurse Henry introduced me. "How do you do?" he said pleasantly, then reverted to his inward conversation. "No, please," he said to the voices there. "Not now. Don't be silly. Oh my God, please don't do that…"

VII

It was 92 degrees and humid as I walked back to the hotel along the desolate bike path and entered the woods. Though only thirty yards wide, it was dense, and adequate cover for predators, human or otherwise. At the very edge of the woods near the hospital lawn was a vacant, dilapidated building which had surrendered to the onslaught of vines, weeds, and briars. The windows and doorway were boarded shut. There was the rank smell of piss and mold as I approached. Crumpled beer cans and shards of glass were strewn about the front. I tried to circle around to the back but got caught in a thorn patch. Making my way back to the bike trail, I made a mental note to revisit this site soon.

That evening I met David Thompson, who had accepted my invitation for dinner and drinks at the hotel. We took a booth in a corner where we could talk and still hear the band. I learned that he was born in Phillipsberg, and had strong feelings about his hometown, despite the economic downturn of late. While everyone took a hit, the poor black project areas felt it the most, and crime was on the rise. He explained to me that, because he was black, he was the department's designated diplomat—the one to go into tough neighborhoods and act as a kind of negotiator and gatherer of information.

I learned also that David Thompson was also a lover of architecture, and that he had studied at Duke for a couple years before coming home to care for his mother and grandmother. He was eager to share his knowledge of the history of the Brown Building, which housed the Phillipsberg Psychiatric Center.

"The Brown building was designed and built by William Mattingly in 1837, who lived right here in Phillipsberg. Mattingly was several years ahead of the renowned architect H.H. Richardson, and had studied in France during the 1850's. Like Richardson, he was big on ancient Roman designs, and some argue that he, more so than Richardson, was responsible for the Romanesque revival movement in America.

"So Mattingly was hired by the city's mayor, Gaylord Brown, who agreed to pay him a lot of money to build a great hospital. Brown, who had inherited a fortune from his family's tobacco industry, wanted a building that would bring international attention to Phillipsberg. He thought he could attract the greatest medical people in America. Brown's dream was to build the centerpiece for American medical research. They put shovels in the ground in 1858 and had nearly completed it when the Civil War broke out. Mattingly enlisted, and was killed the same year. The Brown Building was put on hold until after the war, when one of Richardson's students agreed to finish it. Its doors finally opened in 1869 with a lot of fanfare. For several years it functioned as Phillipsberg's only hospital.

"It is, as you can see, an amazing piece of architecture. The high pointed steeple, the rounded, multi-textured stone walls, the colonettes, the arched doorways and window casings, the balcony—this was all stuff attributed to Richardson and his bold, individualistic style. But it was really Mattingly who set it all in motion.

"The problem was that even though the building appeared impressive, there were a lot of structural flaws that involved costly repair work. It was hard to heat consistently and presented a lot of other logistical problems. More efficient facilities had been designed and were being built in the city. Eventually the whole building was vacant except as a storage area for supplies during the two World Wars. Construction companies lobbied to have it razed. Thankfully, the National Historical Society got involved and managed to preserve it.

"Of course, there were hundreds of wives' tales about the building—ghost stories, murders, tortures in the tower, cannibalism, you know, all the sensational stuff. In the 1950's, part of it was used as a job training center for handicapped people. Then about fifteen years ago, with help of a big grant from the state government and the National Historical Society, it was reconverted to a hospital—our Phillipsberg Psychiatric Center."

Later, as he was leaving, I asked about the small, dilapidated building at the edge of the woods. David Thompson paused, as if reluctant to talk about it, then replied, "That place was built in the 1850's as a school for children with various disabilities like blindness, deafness, mental illness, deformities. It closed just before the Civil War, and has stood there as an eyesore ever since."

VIII

I waited at the front entrance the next morning as Doctor Fredericks arrived in her silver BMW 5. She was preoccupied when I met her at the door. I asked several routine questions, and I sensed some anxiety when I asked about the types of medication typically prescribed here. She pointed me to the pharmacy—a small room down the hall across from the kitchen. Mr. Austry, the pharmacist, would help me.

Austry was an odd little man—pudgy, balding, with thick glasses and a quick, nervous demeanor. He immediately launched into detailed descriptions of all different kinds of antidepressants, barbiturates, and amphetamines, and even vitamin supplements typically used at the hospital. Austry was more than happy to go on sharing his knowledge, to the point where I had to interrupt him mid-sentence several times to clarify what really amounted to too much information. At length, I excused myself and left the pharmacy wondering if he indulged in some of the pills he doled out to the patients.

When I asked for Nurse Henry, security guard Seacrest informed me that she was under the weather, but would return to work tomorrow. It was just then that David Thompson arrived in haste. "Mr. James," he said. "You need to come with me."

IX

The unbloodied body of Mr. Tomkins, the scowling little maintenance worker I met previously, lay prostrate beneath a tree just within the woods, about twenty feet from the bike path. The crime scene had been cordoned off, and two police dogs had been brought in, but they seemed confused, running in circles. Again there was no evidence at the scene other than the needle that was stuck in the buttock of the victim.

As I returned to the hotel that evening, I was surprised to find the pharmacist, Mr. Austry, in the lobby waiting for me. "Inspector James, may we speak in private?"

In my room Mr. Austry continued. "There is something I didn't tell you at the center today, and it is something that may put my job at risk, but I think you need to know. For some reason I don't fully understand, our hospital receives what seems to me an excessive supply of oxycodone every month. I store it in a locked cabinet behind my counter. Three months ago a portion of the supply went missing, along with a case of Novocain and, oddly, a box of jars of liquid fish oil vitamin supplements. I know that medicine security is my responsibility, but I have no idea how someone could have gotten in there. There are only a handful of people who have access to that room. Please understand, Mr. James. I am here to come clean on this, and whatever happens down the road, I hope you can believe that I was not part of it."

After assuring Mr. Austry that I believed him, I decided to return to the hospital. It was near dusk, and the bike path was deserted as I crossed under the canopy of the woods to the lawn at the far end of the hospital property. The crime scene remained cordoned off, the bright yellow ribbons glinting in the light of the half-moon which loomed equidistantly between the jagged tower of the Brown building and the vine-strangled schoolhouse. A quick gust of warm wind turned up the leaves of the vines, and it seemed for a moment as if the school lurched toward me. Suddenly I felt nauseous and dizzy. I hurried along the path toward the hospital and arrived at the back door, fatigued and sweating. "Mr. James," said a familiar voice. "Are you OK?"

X

David Thompson helped me into the building and into a chair in the lobby. I assured him that I was fine, that I am prone to dizzy spells, which always pass in a short while. David looked at me doubtfully, and we sat quietly until the spell had passed.

He then confessed that he had not told me everything about the schoolhouse, and he urged me to follow him upstairs to the fourth floor to meet someone with an important story. "She is hard to understand, Mr. James. Her speech is garbled, and she has problems keeping her focus. But I'd like you to hear this slice of Phillipsberg history coming from someone who is part of it."

David's grandmother rested peacefully in her bed as we entered. It has often occurred to me that, as people grow older, they become less black or white or whatever color. It's as if, as they get closer to God—who is the Great Equalizer—they see themselves less and less as members of a particular clan or race or army. Maybe they have started to understand that for one's soul to enter the Kingdom of heaven, it must first embrace the wholeness of humanity, with all its vice and virtue.

With David there to help translate her drawling southern black accent, I learned his grandmother, Ruth, was a descendant of a line of Georgia slaves who fled to the North before the Civil War via the underground railroad. Ruth's great grandmother, Mabel, and her son and two daughters followed secret instructions leading them along a route of designated safe stations from Wilmington to Greenville. One of the stations was right here in Phillipsberg at the handicap school. They arrived at night, escorted by a freed slave, one who claimed to be an abolitionist. The man, however, was a traitor and a mercenary. He led them into a trap, and the slave catchers came for them at the school.

Then, in the basement of that schoolhouse, the unspeakable happened. The boy was chained up and dragged away, sold off most likely. Mabel and her older daughter were beaten as they were being chained together. During the commotion Mabel hollered to the younger daughter, Hattie, urging her to run for her life. Hattie eluded the slave catchers and managed to escape to the outskirts of Phillipsberg, where she came upon a cabin inhabited by two old slaves. They took Hattie in and protected her identity by sending her to stay with relatives in New York until after the war. Those relatives raised her as their own, and later sent her to college. The girl who escaped the slave catchers was Ruth's grandmother.

The schoolhouse was never designated officially as a part of the underground railroad. It remained a dirty secret among those who employed the slave catchers, and for the blacks who knew the story it was a place of infamy, something to be forgotten.

As I gazed from my window at the dark tower of the Brown Building, a light went suddenly on in my head: Ruth had said the "basement" of the schoolhouse. Suddenly it all made sense. The schoolhouse was only one part of the underground connection. Just before the war, construction had stopped on the Brown building. But the foundation would have been dug as the first part of the construction process, probably followed by the floor and walls of the first story. Also, the roads that were built to handle the supply wagons would have been abandoned, offering a major head start to the North for the runaway slaves. There must be a connection between the two buildings, and it must be literally underground…

XI

The following morning, I found Nurse Henry in the lobby getting ready to start her shift. Reluctantly, she agreed to have coffee with me. Her interest piqued as I explained my theory that there must be an entrance to a tunnel somewhere in the basement of the building. And then, when I abruptly and clumsily asked her if she'd like to have dinner some evening, she flatly refused. "Nothing personal, Mr. James," she said sadly. "And I mean, nothing *personal*. But thank you anyway."

Humbled, I went back to work. I called David and requested a team to search the basement. By late afternoon, they had completed the search, which revealed nothing – no signs of hidden doors or false walls. Just metal, iron, and concrete. All ducts led upward into the building's interior.

Later that night, as I re-envisioned the original structure of the building, it suddenly hit me: the first-floor annex, the ward that held the most seriously psychotic patients, was the first shelter to be built on this sight, months before the main hospital back in the 1850s. Therefore, it must have had its own foundation separate from the main building, and maybe even its own separate cellar or crawlspace. There must be a connection!

I called David immediately, hoping he could meet me at the hospital right away. But he had been called to an emergency in the projects. It was after ten that night as I jogged along the path through the woods and onto the hospital lawn. I paused at the schoolhouse, where I glimpsed something shiny on the ground near the door. There in the brambles was an empty bottle of fish oil. I realized this was the proverbial "red herring" that threw the hounds off track. They smelled fish more than anything else; thus they were unable to follow the scent of the killer.

There was no security guard at the nurses' station as I entered the first ward. Molly, the deaf cleaning woman, was in an agitated state. Making painful attempts to mouth words, she motioned toward room 104, and then 102. William Barnes III, the germaphobe, and Annie, the black woman with the necklace, were gone. In a mad search for a hidden door, I began waking the remaining patients, moving beds and dressers and tables and medical machines. Nothing. Finally, I remembered the mop closet. And there it was, hinged to the floor: a trap door!

The door led down to a crawl space about five feet high, and then to a tunnel narrowing to about five feet in width, at the far end of which shone a dim light. My memory begins to blur at this point. The air was stifling, almost unbreathable, and the place smelled like chemicals and stale dirt. Crouching down and using the light from my key fob, I walked for what must have been fifty yards, passing discarded syringes and empty medicine bottles. There were several small animal traps, some containing dead or half-starved rats that squealed at me as I passed them. At last I entered a small room, almost like a cell, where a short stairway led upward to the source of the light. As I climbed up, I suddenly realized where I was. It was the inside of the schoolhouse, a classroom, with small chairs and desks. That was when the dreams flooded over me. I heard the sobbing of the children, I saw the blood, and my head began to spin out of control.

It was as if the nightmare had become real. As I lay paralyzed on the floor, something was kicking me violently. I looked up to see the crazed eyes of a giant man with a needle in his hand standing over me.

The last thing I remember before all went black was a vision of a small figure glowing in a green light rushing toward me from behind the huge man. Then there was the sound of him screaming hysterically as he clutched at his own neck. "You filthy rotten little bitch!" were his last words he fell on top of me.

XII

A week later, David Thompson came to see me at Phillipsberg Medical Hospital, where I was being treated for minor injuries and a recurring fever accompanied by delusional behavior. He informed me that William "Billy" Barnes had been busy as the devil down there in the underground tunnel. Police had uncovered a large stash of oxycodone and Novocain there, along with a case of syringes and various paraphernalia used to mix the drugs.

There would be an investigation into the hospital employees, proceeding with the theory that the germaphobe Barnes had colluded with the maintenance man, Tomkins, in stealing the drugs from the pharmacy, and later Barnes killed Tompkins, either to shut him up or just for the thrill of it.

The investigation also revealed that the amount of oxycodone the police confiscated at the school was much less than what was unaccounted for over the past several months, according to the pharmacist's records. There was a larger case being built tracing the hospital oxycodone to the oxycodone on the city streets, a case that could implicate high level administrators, including Dr. Fredericks.

When I asked about Annie, the missing woman, he seemed evasive. "I don't know exactly what happened in that schoolhouse," he said. "The obvious scenario would be that Barnes attacked you, there was a fight, you stabbed him with his own weapon, which was the needle, and afterwards you passed out. But I know you don't believe that, and I don't either, not really. I mean, there was not much of a sign of struggle on your part—no torn clothing, no blood, just a few bruises liked you'd been kicked pretty good in your ribs. But not like an all-out fight. And that big Barnes fella, no marks on him except that needle in the back of his neck. How could you have possibly done that?" He paused, looking out the window.

"It's all pretty strange," he continued, displaying now a Rubik's cube on the light tan-colored inside of his elegant, brown hand. The cube had been solved. "We found this in Barnes' room. Appears he was no dummy."

With his other hand, he reached into his pocket, then dangled in front of me the necklace with the hourglass pendant. "And I was wondering about this. After I pulled you out onto the lawn, I found it around your neck. Can you explain?"

I assured him that I could not.

"Well," said David Thompson finally. "All I know is that the little woman from room 102 is gone. She just disappeared, vanished without a trace except for this, which as you know, belonged to her. As I understand it, our Little Orphan Annie has always been a big mystery." David sighed, and seemed to smile just a bit. "So, I guess all we can do now is file a missing-persons report, and then keep our eyes open. Meanwhile, do you think we can close your case as, let's say, a matter of self-defense?"

I assured him that we could.

XIII

That evening, as I was packing my things at the hotel, there was a knock on my door. Like an emerald apparition, Nurse Henry appeared there on the threshold in a green silk dress that caressed her body at every curve. "May I come in, Mr. James"

"I am sorry if I was not as forthcoming as I could have been," she explained. "You see, my husband, who was a musician, died last year. A few years earlier, he was in a car accident, which cracked one of his vertebrae. He had trouble dealing with pain, especially while trying to play the guitar, and he got caught up in the world of pain killers. I knew he had a big problem, but there was nothing I could do. He was out there, doing his thing, on the road much of the time. I never knew where he got his drugs from—prescriptions would have been too expensive, and too restrictive... To make the long story short, our marriage was falling apart. And, though I hate to admit it, I was relieved when he died of an overdose.

"But that's not why I'm here, Mr. James...May I call you Paul? You see, I was, and always will be, a music lover. There is a good band playing downstairs, and I was hoping you would join me for a drink or two?"

Dressing for a Funeral

I

Having been treated to some very good wine and hors d'oeuvres, the twenty-two guests were now cautiously descending the wide and elegant staircase of *Imagone Funeral Home* to the main parlor on the first floor. A spring snowstorm was fussing outside, with large flakes blowing every which way under a darkening late-afternoon sky. Although the wine had tempered some of their misgivings about this strange ordeal, these people had come to Western New York unprepared to deal with this rude stranger who was now rattling the large windows of the home. While some made their complaints openly, others ducked behind attempts at cynical humor. It was clear that all of them were now wishing that this was over so they could return to their more comfortable places in life elsewhere.

In the low lamplight at the far end of the spacious parlor, two elegant ivory caskets seemed to float there among the tiers of bouquets—lilies, orchids, and white roses all provided by the church. There was a hush among the crowd as Mr. Thomas Clarion, the mortician who was filling in for the absent director Roger Alkins, took his place between the two coffins, feeling more like a game show host than an undertaker. "Ladies and gentlemen, friends and family members," he announced rather dramatically, "I have the very unusual, and I should add, very unorthodox task of reading to you the last will and testaments of Maria Alvarez and Harold Kinski."

II

Father John Green stood among the crowd at Buffalo Niagara Airport baggage claim wearing an Hawaiian shirt featuring large, loud parrots and holding a sign above his head that read SEEK AND YE SHALL FIND.

The colorful priest was a slight man, no more than 130 pounds, with receding brown hair and wide-open eyes that seemed not to blink often enough. He greeted me enthusiastically, taking my hand in both of his, which were small and soft. Father Green was one of those men whose exuberance and playful demeanor make it difficult (and probably irrelevant) to try to pin an age on him.

"Mr. James," he exclaimed. "You have found me. Welcome to Buffalo!"

It was a dim and grey Monday morning in April as Father Green drove from the airport to Lackawanna, home to the national shrine *Our Lady of Victory Basilica*. The priest, who was from Buffalo originally, was proud to have been assigned here at this mid-point in his life-service to God. He spoke with the authority of one who has traveled the world, claiming that Buffalo was a blessed place indeed—the notorious lake effect winter storms symbolizing mankind's internal and external struggles, while the lush and peaceful summers and autumns remind us of Pope Pius V's victory over the Ottomans, and of the strength and hope that can be achieved through prayer. He was a man of deep, unequivocal faith.

III

Flanked by copper topped twin spires, the great dome of *Our Lady of Victory Basilica* rose 120 feet into the sky. Four giant angels, each eighteen feet tall, trumpeted from the dome's rim. The adjunct colonnades boasted their own guardian angels, each tending to a group of children clamoring for enlightenment. Encased in a domed niche above the main entrance was the twelve-foot marble statue of the *Lady* herself. Among these giants, there was, in effect, an ambience of great mystery—the edifice seemed to emanate its own light from a source within, a light greater than that of the grey sky of South Buffalo on this early spring day.

As we walked across the parking lot toward the church, there was a shout from behind. "Father," hollered a slightly hunched man with a US Marine-style brush cut and wire-rim glasses. He pointed accusingly at the priest's car. "If you leave it like that, with its rear end sticking out, someone will hit it. You know it's happened before, and it will happen again."

"Oh shit, what a pain" said the good priest under his breath, excusing himself to go and pull his car up several inches so that it was out of harm's way.

As we approached the front entrance to the basilica we were accosted by a quick and wiry little lady with blue hair. "Father John," she pleaded. "I ask you again: can't you find some way to quiet that child at the 10:00 mass. And I'm not the only one complaining. For God's sake, we can't even hear your homily above that wretched crying. It happens every week. And those parents, who are barely adults themselves, they have no control over it." Having cut us off from entry, she continued her protest. "And don't forget that there are many parishioners who are concerned about the bingo schedule changing. It has always been on Tuesdays."

The priest took her by her mottled, knobby hands and explained apologetically and earnestly. "Milly, you know that God's house is open to all comers, and I have neither the authority nor the heart to turn people away. And as for bingo, the bishop wants us to try Thursday. He feels that we might draw more people later in the week. But when I speak with him I will let him know of your concerns."

The interior of the Basilica was even more magnificent than the exterior. A host of six-foot tall white marble angels stood like sentinels throughout the church, some holding fonts, some ushering in the aisles, others engaged in their guardianship of the innocent. Along the walls, the Stations of the Cross were also human-sized, and the drama of Christ's Crucifixion, frozen in white, seemed as if it might breathe life at any moment.

The Great Dome's ceiling was painted with images of the Coronation, the Assumption, the twelve apostles and three archangels, along with Jesus in a scarlet red robe. A white dove of peace signaled His ascent to heaven.

Most mesmerizing to me were the sixteen stained glass windows that formed a ring around the dome's mural. These portals of multi-colored light hovered there like an alignment of glowing planets, leaving the impression that what lies out there beyond this life is, at the same time, already right here before us and within reach.

The mahogany pews, with a seating capacity of 1,200, were mostly empty as we walked up the aisle toward the apse. Suddenly I noticed in one of the pews an elderly woman lying in a crumpled heap, half her body on the seat, the other half on the floor! Father John seemed not to notice, so I exclaimed, "Father, that woman might be dead!"

The priest paused, regarding the woman with a tinge of impatience. Then he shook the pew rather harshly, after which the woman regained consciousness and, seeming at once both annoyed and desperate, began sputtering, "Jesus Mary and Joseph! God take me, please."

"Myrtle," said the priest. "It is not your time yet. God will call when He's ready for you." Under his breath he said to me, "I'm not sure He will ever be ready for her."

To the right of the altar a younger man stood waving one hand urgently at the priest while pointing the other at the confessional booth. As Father John approached, the man tried to speak, stuttering and stammering—something about the devil following him, making him do bad things. The Priest informed him that today was Monday, and confession was not until Saturday. He then reassured the nervous little man that this devil was indeed an impostor, without any powers, and that he shouldn't worry.

A door by the apse led us down a set of stairs into the basement. Having some church business to attend to, Father Green excused himself, allowing me some time to visit the museum. A half hour later I was greeted by one of the church's altar boys, who led me through a long corridor and up a staircase to meet the Father in his living quarters, an adjoining building that had at one time been part of the Our Lady of Victory Orphanage. We sat in the living room of the rectory. "So, Mr. James, as you know, these are strange waters we are navigating here. I am happy to help you in your investigation, but as I'm sure you are already aware there are some places I can't go—priestly duties, matters of trust, as you know."

IV

We were joined shortly by police officer Johnson, who had conducted the initial investigation. From him I learned that the strange incident which brought me here to Buffalo occurred last Friday at *Memory Lane,* a home for seniors who are in the final stages of their particular brand of dementia. A man, Harold Kinski, and a woman, Maria Alvarez, both having turned 90 years old that very same day, were found dead in their respective beds on the third floor across the hall from each other. Their birthdays were their death days.

Aside from the birthday coincidence, there were two strange occurrences: Harold and Maria died almost simultaneously, their oxygen kits beeping within minutes. The night staff was apparently a bit slow getting there, but the nurse on duty reported having seen a quick figure slipping through the door to the stairway. She also described a smell that reminded her of a science lab. Most strange was the fact that their sheets had been pulled off them and their gowns removed, leaving their bodies in their "birthday suits." Reluctantly, the officer added that both the deceased residents seemed to be smiling.

Not surprising was that most of their small possessions—those trivial yet symbolic items left by friends and family members on the nightstands to adorn the otherwise empty and sterile environs of the hospital rooms—were missing. All that remained in the nightstand drawers were cheap, abridged versions of the Bible (supplied by Memory Lane), plastic rosary beads, church bookmarkers, and a handful of old black and white photographs that were either torn or stained and blurry. These items were given to me as the only bits of evidence obtained by the police. The officer assured me that his team had found no forensic evidence—no prints or hairs or anything useful in that regard.

Following our briefing session, Father Green showed me to my quarters at the far end of the rectory. The room was small and not well-lit, but quaint—the walls papered with green and gold leaves falling gently from graceful branches. Above my bed was a large portrait of Jesus praying in the Garden, red tears falling from his incredibly dark and forlorn eyes. This was a powerful image, one that conveyed profound sadness and suffering while at the same time offering consolation and inspiration. In the sanctity of this place, I felt sheltered from the dreams that have haunted me since the school massacre years ago.

V
_____

That evening I visited Memory Lane, a bland, sprawling two-story structure built in the 70's. Operated by Erie County, the home had been designed for end-of-life care, and apparently aesthetics was not a priority. The walls were white, the windows small and scarce, and overall there was an air of antiseptic and chloride that assaulted the nose. Nevertheless, the medical staff members were cooperative and, it seemed, excited to be of help as I questioned them thoroughly about the events of last Friday midnight.

By all accounts, the two residents had been in limbo for quite a while. Like most patients in this place, what was tethering them to this world had frayed to the finest last bits of thread. Regarding the photographs from their drawers, no one was able to identify any of the people posing, although one older nurse claimed that she recognized the beach setting in one photo as Evangola State Park. No one except for the nurse on duty—the one who claimed to see a stranger in the hallway—could think of anything out of the ordinary over the past several weeks or months.

According to several employees, the only visitor to Alvarez and Kinski had been a man of cloth, so to speak—an unsociable sort who made the rounds reciting the Lord's Prayer to many of the patients, undeterred by their apparent oblivion. Looking at the visitor sign-in register, I discovered the name Pastor Parker Hole, who apparently came once a week, usually on a Thursday. One of the nurses described him as wearing a hat over his long dark hair, a beard, and thick glasses. He appeared more a rabbi than a reverend.

Regarding the missing items from the nightstands, none of the staff could remember exactly what those items were, nor could they recall the visitors who brought them to the rooms. Moreover, there were many discrepancies in their accounts of what the objects were. In the case of Ms. Alvarez, a nurse's aide claimed that there was a white plastic horse, or maybe it was a unicorn, she wasn't certain. Another aide seemed to recall a miniature statue of Jesus, the kind with a magnet used to adhere to an old car's metal dashboard, but then again maybe that belonged to the other woman who passed away a few weeks before... One nurse definitely recalled a Christmas snow globe that over time had begun to leak and was thrown out. As if by magic, the objects seemed to change on a regular basis, claimed one cleaning woman.

As for Mr. Kinski, there was a similar lack of consensus. A plastic hourglass (a gift that might be deemed a cruel joke in this place), a vase with fake roses, an old picture frame with a colored photo of a porch featuring someone whose age and gender were uncertain in the grainy-ness of it all.

Nonetheless, what all seemed to remember, and this with respect to both rooms, were swatches of cloth, often held in the hands of the patients at least up until the last few months when the necessary motor skills had abandoned them. The swatches were of high quality—silk or satin, very smooth and shiny, like material from very expensive clothing. However, there was much contradiction regarding both the number and the colors of the pieces of cloth. No one was really sure.

VI

On Tuesday, I went to the office of public records. I learned that Mr. Kinski graduated from Lackawanna High School in 1934. He was a retired Bethlehem Steel worker. His pension was considerable, yet he chose to live in the neighborhood of Lackawanna, where he was born in 1915. He served as a cook in WWII, after which he never married. He had one brother, who died over twenty years ago leaving one daughter, who was a very successful realtor living in New York City. Kinski was a lifelong *Our Lady of Victory* parishioner, and a generous donor.

Ms. Alvarez, the daughter of migrant workers from Mexico, moved permanently to South Buffalo when her father got a job at Bethlehem Steel. She graduated from Lackawanna high school in 1935. She never married, and there was no record of children born to her. She was predeceased by a brother, whose son had become a wealthy evangelist in Dallas, Texas. Her early career was sketchy, but she ended up working for New Era Hat Company and retired with a nice pension. She was also a life-long parishioner at *OLV*.

Besides graduating from the same school and attending the same church, I discovered three other commonalities: Their bodies had been sent to the same mortuary; their last wills were written by the same lawyer during the same month of the same year; they were close neighbors, living in separate apartments of a duplex, which Kinski purchased thirty years ago. They lived in that duplex until last year when they were both transferred to Memory Lane.

Father Green was awake and in a bright mood when I returned to the rectory that evening. We drank wine and talked into the night about small things, yet it seemed that he was looking into my soul, tacitly assuring me that whatever darkness was there could come to light. There was a moment where I felt as if I could reveal my burden, yet I held back. Perhaps after the investigation…

After bidding the good priest goodnight, I returned to my room and reexamined the photos left in the nightstand drawers of the old couple. They were all too liquid-stained, faded, or blurry to be of much use, yet I discovered two pictures, one from each person's belongings, that were remarkable in that both featured three individuals—a man, woman, and child. It was unclear whether the child was a boy or girl. The picture from Mr. Kinski's drawer was set at a beach in the summer, perhaps Evangola State Park as the older nurse had suggested. In Ms. Alvarez' photo, the trio stood in front of a Christmas tree.

VII

The next morning I visited the mortuary—Imagone Funeral Home—owned and operated by Roger Alkins, who had purchased the business several years ago. As I suppose is characteristic of many who have undertaken (no pun intended) this line of work, Mr. Alkins presented himself as the epitome of courtesy and formality. I suppose that projecting an air of such compassion and dignity serves to waylay the general public's morbid preconceptions regarding morticians. Indeed, the kinds of chemicals necessary for the artful and artificial works of morticians may affect their appearance and bearing as they grow older. And although they serve in the same brotherhood with priests and physicians—those in front of whom all men must lay down their arms—morticians are not so much revered; their relationship with the family members is tenuous, requiring a reluctant intimacy on both sides. I imagine morticians must sometimes feel like the red-headed stepchild of God.

Alkins had the precise and delicate carriage of a figure skater. Though probably middle-aged, he had the face of a young model, with light brown hair, sharp nose and chin, arched eyebrows and a gaze that was both compassionate and distant. But what was most remarkable about his appearance was the prominent scar on his lower jaw—a single slit extending from his chin to just below his ear. On this unique face, however, the scar was less a blemish than a distinguishing mark that added to his mysterious beauty.

The mortician was assertive as he engaged me in discussion about the two deceased individuals. He had, in fact, just completed preparing and preserving them for the church service, which was to be held Friday at Father John's behest. He noted that the dressing of the bodies was not a matter of importance, as it had been determined that both would be in closed caskets. He informed me that the caskets had already been sealed, and that after having thoroughly inspected their corpses with the assistance of the coroner, there was nothing unnatural or suspicious about their deaths. It was a mere coincidence that they arrived at his home at the same time in the same ambulance. As we parted, he informed me that he was leaving on vacation the next morning and his friend and fellow mortician, Thomas Clarion, would be in charge of the proceedings from here on.

I then phoned Attorney Debbie Valentine, of Valentine and Associates. She had inherited the practice from her father, Judge Frank Valentine—the man who sealed the wills of both clients over twenty years ago. She informed me over the phone that she visited the clients just two years ago, and that they were both of sound mind and were living unassisted in the duplex on Ridge Road. She had determined that there was no cause to question the wills. Nevertheless, at my request, Ms. Valentine agreed to see me later that afternoon at her office.

Debbie Valentine, who stood a just a little over five feet tall, had short blond hair, full lips, and bright eyes that shone with good humor and genuine enthusiasm.

"I've been waiting for this one," she said, leading me into her office. It was apparent that, as she turned to her file cabinets, she was not timid about displaying her well-rounded figure—her short, tight fitting black skirt inching up one shapely leg as she leaned on the other. "I'm sorry to hear that they have passed, but obviously they lived a full life. My father was their lawyer and their friend," she explained. "He wrote their wills—it must have been over twenty years ago, not long before Dad died. But I remember it well because he often talked about it, in vague terms of course. It was something very interesting to him and seemed to amuse him. He also hinted that there was a lot of money involved." She paused and looked at me, her eyes widening playfully. "And that always makes things more intriguing, don't you agree?"

Sitting down at her desk with the two files, she leaned forward, her purple flowered blouse revealing a marvelous depth of cleavage. (This was a confidant woman!) "So Mr. James," she teased, "shall we have a look-see?"

The first file—that of Mr. Kinski—contained a sealed envelope, which the lawyer opened to reveal a second sealed envelope and an open letter providing specific instructions regarding the reading of the will. On the second envelope was written DO NOT OPEN UNTIL AFTER THE FUNERAL SERVICE.

Ms. Valentine and I looked incredulously at each other from across the table. Then, inviting me to come behind the desk where we could both read, she pulled Ms. Alvarez' file, which contained almost the exact same information and directives!

To summarize, the letters made it clear that 1) all assets would be liquidated, 2) the inheritance would be divided fairly among family members, the church, and an anonymous executor (whose identity was known only to the lawyer and would be revealed in the second envelope), and 3) all family members will be notified immediately and invited to come to the funeral. This would be initiated through contact with the oldest blood relatives of each party: For Kinski it was the wealthy realtor/niece in New York City. For Alvarez, the Texas evangelist. Moreover, a $15,000 fund had been established for airline tickets on a first come, first serve basis until that money was exhausted.

"You know what is so odd?" said Debbie Valentine. "Neither Maria nor Harold had ever even met their niece or nephew."

VIII

Debbie Valentine turned out to provide excellent company for me that evening as we drank and dined at a fine Italian restaurant. Yet despite my compromised condition, I knew it was time to have another talk with Father Green.

He seemed to have anticipated my visit when I returned to the rectory later that night. "Well, then," he said with a sigh. "I suppose it's time you learned more about Harold Kinski and Maria Alverez."

"They were always friends, even in high school. Yet they insisted that they were never intimate partners. They were odd ducks, for certain, and in those days, being odd was tantamount to being queer. They were mocked by classmates in high school, and even their own families regarded them with a measure of contempt. Eventually, both were for all intents and purposes disowned by their families.

"Of course, as birds of a feather, Harold and Maria flew together. As their companionship developed in an unorthodox manner, so did their sense of humor. It is hard for a priest to laugh, but those two might have caused even Jesus Christ Himself to crack a smile. Sometimes I was afraid how far they might push the envelope, but their indiscretions were always slight, and their delivery was so gently naïve.

"Anyway, they *were* queer, I suppose, though not in the modern sense of the word. There was really no "closet" to be in or out of for them. Regardless of how they were treated growing up, they became such kind-hearted and generous people. Whenever there was a person in need at our parish, they were the first in line to help in whatever way they could. They volunteered for the food and clothing drives. They worked the homeless shelters tirelessly. Even in their seventies they managed to help shovel snow at the church during blizzards.

"30 years ago, when they were 60 years old, they went through a lengthy and personally invasive process in an attempt to adopt a child. A particularly mean-spirited social worker was ruthless in her attempts to discredit Harold and Maria, citing age and issues of sexuality as evidence against them. That woman, along with the fact that they weren't married, pretty much ruled them out. Well, that's when I came in, trying to return an ounce for the buckets of kindness they had poured into our church. Oh, I should give some credit to old Judge Frank Valentine—you might have met his lovely daughter Debbie by now? Well, bless old Frank's agnostic heart. He was part of the scheme. So, to make the long story short, Mr. James, we provided the marital documents and the personal references required for them to legally adopt a child.

"In an orphanage near Syracuse they found a 10-year old boy, which is a dangerously late age. As a child, the boy had been mentally and physically abused by his parents, and he still bears the scars that prove it. For the first few years after the adoption, it was a terrible struggle. The boy was an emotional wreck, lashing out at whatever he could, trying to run away back to his friends at the orphanage. But Harold and Maria stuck with him, always forgiving, always finding ways to get through to the next episode.

"Later, as he entered high school, there was a remarkable change, a kind of metamorphosis. During his sophomore year, he grew more self-restrained, more respectful, more thoughtful. He became very popular at school as he developed a personality—it seemed he adopted some of his parents' sense of humor. And he also bloomed as a physical specimen. By the time he was 16, despite his scars, he had offers from fashion magazines in New York City to work as a model.

"The most remarkable thing of all, Mr. James, was that the boy turned down the call to fame in the big city in favor of staying right here in Buffalo with his parents. He loved them so dearly. But a few years ago, as their condition deteriorated and they could no longer care for themselves, he had to put them in that home. It was so hard for him to see them trapped like that, believing their souls had already flown away."

Father Green paused, then smiled dismissively. "I believe you met him this morning. Remarkable, isn't he? And now, forgive me, Mr. James, but I must retire...for the night, I mean. I have a sermon to write before Friday, and, as this is one close to my heart, it will not be an easy task."

IX

The weather forecast for the day of the funeral included the strong likelihood of a lake effect storm, not surprising for Western New York in April. As a measure of precaution, the mortician-in-charge, Thomas Clarion, decided that the caskets should remain in the Home (contrary to Catholic custom of bringing them to the church) until after the service when they would be delivered to the Holy Cross Cemetery for burial.

Among the fifty-odd parishioners who attended the funeral of Harold Kinski and Maria Alvarez, twenty-two had flown into Buffalo on the last-minute free-ticket deal with hopes of getting something more. Very few knew each other, and it was largely a gathering of strangers. Some were not even family members, but rather there as representatives of extended family members. Before the service there was much chatter about the inheritance, some cautiously optimistic, some highly skeptical, some downright cynical (but not above taking a freebie whenever they could get one). One couple claimed that God had shown them the way here from Texas. Many jokes were made at the expense of Buffalo's reputation for losing sports teams and foul weather. There was one, however, who remained quiet throughout. He wore a beard and glasses, always standing apart from the rest while trying to make himself inconspicuous.

Father Green wore a magnificent teal and gold stole adorned with images of the cross as he stood by the alter. The church was bathed in the mystical light coming down from the stained-glass windows of the Great Dome. Despite the modest and mostly non-Catholic turnout, the Father delivered an eloquent and passionate homily in honor of the deceased. These two people were not just parishioners; they had been close friends of the Father for over twenty years since he arrived at the Basilica. Both Harold and Maria possessed great vitality, faith, and spirit, along with unique senses of humor. It was obvious that the Father had loved them, and when the choir began the Communion song, "Miracle of Grace" it seemed that he would break into tears at any moment. However, despite the emotional presentation by Father John, the visitors appeared unmoved, but rather restless to get the affair over with. A scarce few of them received communion, and the Mass seemed to end abruptly.

In conclusion, Father Green made an important announcement. "At the behest of the deceased, there will be a gathering back at the funeral home for members of the family. At that time, matters of the estate will be made public."

X

I stood there in the parlor with Father Green and Debbie Valentine behind the twenty-two relatives of Harold Kinski and Maria Alvarez. Mortician Thomas Clarion, standing in for Roger Alkin, opened the first envelope, the one from Mr. Kinski:

I have instructed our Mortician to, upon dressing me for the last show, place hidden upon my person and within the coffin a specific item of considerable value. When all is said and done, this item will be taken out and revealed to you, my dear cousins.

A murmur went through the crowd—whispers about the closed caskets, about this being a joke of some sort...

Clarion continued, opening the second envelope, this one from the will of Maria. Raising his eyebrows, he read with a voice that was almost musical:

Ditto.

A large, thick-necked man representing the Evangelist Church hollered out in his Texas drawl, "What in God's name is going on here. These coffins are closed, the good lord tells us not to defile those who are at peace. There must be some other way, some copy of the documents somewhere."

"That's right," yelled one of the female delegates from New York City. "The lawyers must have a copy in their possession. They need to step up and take care of this now," she asserted, looking over at Debbie and me.

Mr. Clarion then interjected, saying that there was more in the note from Ms. Alvarez: *P.S. In the event that we have been "closed" from regular viewing, then by all means, open us up and come and get what's there. Otherwise, it gets buried with us. There are no copies.*

And so Mr. Clarion proceeded to unhitch the several brass latches surrounding the cover and open the first coffin. Despite the powerful aroma of formaldehyde, the crowd leaned in cautiously, some covering their nose and mouth with tissues. Then there was a collective gasp as they beheld the object of their morbid curiosity. Lying upon a purple satin fabric of the bedding and dressed in a satin teal-colored tutu with pink leggings was the figure of a man, smiling, thumbs pointed straight in the air, his face painted like a clown's! The mortician, after a brief inspection, removed an envelope protruding from the under the pillow. Inside was a check. His voice rose above the cries of disgust and protest.

"A check made out to the executor for the amount of $200,000.00 has been signed and turned over as a donation to Catholic Charities." This news received unfavorable reviews from the audience, who were growing more and more impatient in anticipation of what was hidden in the other coffin.

Thomas Clarion, seeming to take his role quite dramatically, strode to the other box. There, like a magician on a stage, he slowly opened the lid to reveal the figure of a woman, splendidly outfitted in a cowboy suit, replete with boots, spurs, chaps, jacket, vest, hat (which was a bit crumpled) and even a lone star sheriff's badge on her breast. The material of her suit was a plush gold velvet, and in her hands she held two shiny plastic pistols pointed straight up. Clarion then reached down below her boots and removed a burlap bag—the kind you see in robbery scenes in the old Westerns—filled and tied at the brim. There was a note attached: *For the Families to Divide among Themselves.*

"That's cash money," yelled a man in a business suit. The crowd, whose morbid curiosity had been partially repelled by the smell of chemicals, now moved closer. As the man moved aggressively toward the caskets, the preacher from Texas blocked his progress. Thomas Clarion sensed the urgency of the moment. Closing the caskets with an air of finality, he proposed that three representatives from each family follow him into the back room where they would assess the contents of the bag and distribute equitably.

It was in fact cash money, over a thousand bills. However, what was tragically disappointing to the extended family members was that they were all one-dollar bills. This set off a fresh round of complaint, the most acute of which demanded to know the identity of the executor. And after Clarion told them that it was the owner of Imagone Funeral Home—Mr. Roger Alkins, adopted son of Maria and Harold—the crowd became hostile. A New York representative then threatened a huge lawsuit, claiming that they all had been deceived, emotionally abused, and that she would get to the bottom of the underhanded, unethical lawyering going on in this Podunk town called Buffalo. The crowd quickly dispersed, and no one went to the cemetery for the burial.

Well, almost no one. Debbie Valentine and I waited there for an hour, but the hearse never arrived.

XI

In the meantime, the snow had given up, the sky had turned Egyptian blue, and a scarlet red sun was fading on the Lake Erie horizon. After packing my bags, I took a last walk into the basilica, where I found Father Green sitting in the front pew. "I understand that Ms. Valentine will be taking you to the airport." he said. "Is there anything else I can help you with."

There was, I told him. First, I wanted to know the identity of the man with the black beard and glasses who never spoke to anyone at the church and funeral. The priest told me simply that he does not check everyone's ID who comes to his church.

Then I asked him why he did not go to the cemetery for the burial. After a long silence, the priest sighed deeply. He confessed to me it was all farce. Harold and Maria had been buried days before, and the bodies in the caskets at the funeral home were mannequins. The chemicals odors were sprayed inside the caskets. But the sensational costumes that adorned the mannequins were very real and very precious.

Finally, I wanted to know what he thought the exact cause of death of the old couple really was.

"Mr. James, I am not a coroner. I am a priest, and as such, I cannot tell a lie." Smiling sadly, he walked away past the altar of *Our Lady of Victory*. Then pausing beneath the statue of Mary and her Son, he turned back to me. "By the way, Mr. James, do you think what you wear here, in this life, is more or less important than what you wear after you are gone?"

A Lion in the Woods

I

It was nearly dark when 10-year-old Tommy Tucker zipped around the corner of the old train station and witnessed the cougar atop its prey. Startled by the bicycle's squeaking brakes and flickering headlight, the huge cat retracted its claws and fled across the tracks, disappearing behind an abandoned warehouse. There on the side of the tracks was the limp body of a small girl, face down in the rocky dirt. Her shirt was ripped open, her back and shoulders raked and bloody. But she was alive.

This was the latest of a string of attacks from the mountain lion that had escaped the Erie Zoo a month ago. It turned out that the girl was luckier than many other victims; the carcasses of more than a dozen deer (easy prey in these suburban jungles) along with several dogs were clear evidence of the cat's prowess.

Tommy Tucker was an unlikely hero. The frail, white-haired boy with poor eyesight and a speech impediment somehow managed to convey the emergency to a nearby pedestrian, who called 911. The EMT's, despite having no experience in giant cat attacks, managed to dress the wounds in time to save the little girl.

The girl, Jasmine Johnson, lived a few blocks from those tracks in a small, under-furnished house, part of a project development in which drug dealing and turf battles were becoming a way of life. Recent layoffs at the nearby Electric General plant had exacerbated the situation. Too many young adults now had idle time on their hands, and the drug markets had penetrated the public schools.

Jasmine was the stereotypical child in those neighborhoods—absent father, overworked mother, and an older brother who, despite having shown promise in school as a talented athlete and artist, was running with a gang.

She was a curious, wide-eyed little girl who liked to wear her hair in twisted braids with pink picks on top. With so little supervision, she became prone to wandering farther and farther from her home. It was her misfortune to have been hunting for specimens for her bug collection by the tracks on the evening the cougar was prowling there.

I came to Erie to investigate the cause of the animal's escape, which was the subject of much debate. My agency had instructed me to initiate a plan, in conjunction with zoo officials and local police, to capture the cat alive. Zoo spokespersons had initially tried to downplay the urgency of the situation, fearing a hyped-up media response and the public outcry from animal rights activists, who had been successful in convincing police that the animal was born in captivity, and consequently would not have developed killer instincts. The cat was relatively young (just a year and a half old) and small (110 pounds). She would certainly avoid contact with humans until she was nearly starving.

That was the story until the attack on the girl, after which everything changed. Now there was extensive news coverage, with broadcasters repeating conspiracy theories from the locals about how the animal got loose and why the zoo officials were not forthcoming. Then there was talk of a big reward for bagging the cat, and despite warnings from the police, local vigilante groups gathered behind closed doors to oil their guns and plan their strategies.

II

The railyard where the girl was attacked was just three miles from the zoo. After WW II, Electric General, the giant power factory near the shores of Lake Erie, anticipated the need for more rails as the city's population and its demand for energy increased. The company bought thousands of acres of unused land. However, as the city highway system expanded during the 1960's, more and more tractor trailers were being used for general transportation. Roads were built, and the localized iron spurs became less used. By the end of the next decade, most of the rails were obsolete. They had rusted over and were now subject to the relentless encroachment of weeds and brush. The result was more than five square miles of ragged, untamed wilderness separating the factories from the suburbs of Erie. Thickets of sumac, locusts, water willows and silver maples, with their attendant grape vines and poison ivy patches, now dominated the landscape. The rusted tracks and dilapidated warehouses stood among them as symbols of wasted ambition.

Farther away from the tracks and interspersed across the acres of the brush and dwarf woods were several stands of larger, older trees that had escaped the original commercial land development of Electric General. These were mature forests of oak, beech, birch, tulip, red maples, and evergreens indigenous to the Lake Erie coastal region, now looming above the landscape like dark fortresses.

During the eighties, the state government purchased much of the abandoned property from E.G. It was a sweet deal for the city and for the company. The EPA somehow overlooked the numerous chemical spills that had occurred in the yards, and both state and federal grants were readily approved to expedite the development. In what was heralded as a progressive move by the city council, portions of the area were razed and redeveloped as residential zones for low income people, who would move there in hopes of escaping urban crime. It was named Bainesville, after the Pennsylvania House Representative Harvey Baines, who invested generously in the project. However, because of their geographic isolation (four miles from the city) and recent defunding of the police department, the neighborhoods gradually became a breeding ground for gangs.

What added to the volatility of Bainesville was its proximity to a town at the opposite edge of the wilderness: Pleasantville, a rural village before the city's expansion, was now a largely white, lower middle-class suburban community. Running in a straight line through the fields and patches of forest that separated the two towns was a single, two-mile long rail spur. Though this was the private property of E.G., it was unpatrolled, and trespassers, mostly teenagers, had worn several paths through the fields and woodlands.

Tensions had grown between the communities over the years. Bainesville had become a real bane in the eyes of Pleasantville citizens. Every crime that occurred in Pleasantville was blamed on someone from Bainesville. Now, with a vicious wild animal on the loose, along with a recently authorized $2000.00 reward for its capture dead or alive, the land separating the two communities had become a whole new jungle, and racial tensions were growing.

As I perused the google earth maps of the areas surrounding Bainesville, Pleasantville, the Erie Zoo, and the Electric General Plant, it occurred to me that, if I were a fugitive seeking refuge, it would be within those older forests, the great stands of oak and maple and beech trees that blotted the map in dark green. But that would come later. My first job was to interrogate the staff that worked at the zoo.

III

I began with Head Keeper Harold Comden, who was visibly upset over the whole ordeal. According to Comden, it happened at night with the animals locked inside their cages, when only the second shift, nonprofessional workers were on duty to clean the outdoor areas. He was certain that there was meddling, that someone had opened the latches to the cage. Furthermore, the night lights by both the cat complex and front entrance had been knocked out by someone, probably with a slingshot or by throwing rocks. Surveillance cameras showed one indistinguishable, shadowy figure hurrying toward the cat complex.

"I have no idea how or why someone would have opened that cage," said Harold Comden. "It doesn't make any sense. I know my professional staff, and they are all highly trained men and women. They are reliable and ethically sound, or I wouldn't have hired them. I can't think of any reason someone would want to harm the animals, or to put the community in danger. As far as the support staff goes, they have no access to the entry codes. The whole thing is just plain crazy."

I asked the zookeeper about the escaped lion's history.

"Bellatrix was pure cougar—or mountain lion or puma, whatever you want to call them—it's all the same species. Anyway, she was born two weeks premature about eighteen months ago. The birthing happened in the early morning hours, with the skeleton crew of night-shifters on duty and only one in the cat complex. Because the night shift veterinarian had recently been fired, there was no readily available professional medical assistance, and by the time an emergency crew arrived, the mother, Medusa, had managed to give birth to three kits. One of the three was stillborn, and we had a hell of a time getting it out of the cage with mom in such a nasty mood.

"Medusa was wild-caught. She was mean-tempered, even for a puma, and showed signs early that she was reluctant to nourish the cubs, at times appearing to pose a danger to them. So the two surviving cubs, both females, were taken away from her as soon as we could get them out of there. One was sold to the Buffalo Zoo, the other, Bellatrix, was kept here in Erie and reared by staff members. Temperament-wise, she was a lot like her mother. Despite being raised by humans, she had grown into a restless and moody cat. I can tell you one thing for sure, Mr. James. That cat may be young and not yet full grown, but she is a mean one."

After interviewing all the professional staff, including behaviorists, biologists, nutritionists, and veterinarians, I had to agree with Comden; these were knowledgeable specialists in their respective fields, and all seemed equally baffled by the breach of security.

The nonprofessional, support staff was not as cooperative. Their job description included feeding the animals according to prescribed diets, facilitating their movement among the different sections of their confined areas, cleaning their excrement, and assisting the professional staff in sedating or anesthetizing the animals for medical or behavior issues. It occurred to me that they were acutely aware of the difference between their near minimum wage and the bloated salaries of the specialists, and they knew their jobs were never quite secure in this environment where anything that goes wrong can readily be blamed on those at the bottom. They were defensive, ready to deliver stock answers in anticipation of becoming somebody's scapegoat.

I gleaned little from them, but I was intrigued by one young man named Jimmy Tucker, the older brother of the white-haired boy who witnessed the cougar attack. Normally Jimmy worked the day shift, but had volunteered for overtime, and, as it turns out, was alone in the cat complex when the cubs were born. He was 18 years old now, very thin, freckled, with bright red hair and flickering green eyes that would not meet mine. He claimed he was nervous watching Medusa and the newborns, but there was nothing he could do but call the zoo hotline. When asked about the night of the escape, he said he was not on duty. Despite his alibi, it occurred to me that if anyone knew something about what happened that night, it was Jimmy Tucker.

IV

On Tuesday morning I phoned the mother of Jasmine Johnson requesting an interview with her daughter in an effort to gain more information that might serve us in our efforts to capture the cougar. At first she was angry, going off on some rant about how irresponsible the zoo, the police, and the whole city had been. She told me there was no way for her to get to the zoo any way, and the best thing I could do was make sure someone shot that cat dead soon. However, she softened as I questioned about Jasmine's health after what must have been a traumatic experience. Eventually she agreed to let me come to her house that evening.

As I drove from the city at dusk, the October sunset over Lake Erie was magnificent. A thin, darkening ribbon stretched across the far edge where the sky merged with the lake. Orange and purple cirrocumulus clouds hovered above, covering the lake like a glowing warm blanket. The horizon faded, then intensified to a deep red ember, soon to be extinguished and followed by a moment of ubiquitous green light.

It was dark when I exited the freeway and headed south on Baines Road toward the Johnson home. The road ran parallel to a spur of old tracks. There was inadequate streetlighting in Bainseville, a piece of civil engineering overlooked by the ambitious developers and their pursuit of shortcuts to complete the project within budget restrictions. Yet I could see the housing projects that sprawled north and south along the road—mostly two-story quads surrounded by parking lots and square, grassy lawns and small playgrounds.

The woman who answered the door introduced herself as Jade Johnson. She appeared nervous, impatient, perhaps embarrassed as she invited me into her humble apartment. She was still in her uniform from the nursing home in the city where she had worked overtime hours. But I could see that she was a very attractive woman with a well-rounded, strong figure; I felt that she was the kind of woman whose intensity and defensiveness might, in times less stressful, give way to a soft and warm allure.

She brought me a bottle of water and instructed me to sit in the living room while she fetched Jasmine from the playground. The room was clean and neat, but barely furnished, with only a couch, a chair, a TV, and a couple end tables, each with a jade plant. On the walls, however, were two remarkable oil paintings. One was of an old locomotive resembling the Union Pacific, with dark clouds of steam billowing from the stacks as it roared toward a range of stormy mountains. The other was very different in mood, featuring two boats on a tranquil sea.

As I perused the paintings, a young man of 16 or 17 years old with dread-locks came hurriedly from a bedroom. It was clear he had urgent business at hand, as he barely acknowledged my presence. He grabbed a jacket from a closet and, closing the door quietly, was gone into the night.

A minute later Ms. Johnson returned with Jazmine. "Bobby?" she called toward the room the boy had just exited. "Oh Lord," she said, shaking her head. "What am I going to do with that boy?" She went out the front door, to look for him, leaving me alone with Jasmine

Initially, Jasmine was timid and reluctant to speak with me. But she warmed gradually as I questioned her about school and friends, and she especially brightened when I asked about her older brother Robert, to whom she seemed deeply connected. At length, she revealed the basic situation of her encounter with the cat: she was searching for bugs by the tracks when she suddenly was pinned down face first by something heavy and strong. Then she felt the pain—a stabbing sensation in her back and arms. It all happened so fast. She never actually saw the beast, and apparently she was in a state of shock when the ambulance arrived.

V

It was about 7:00 when I said goodnight to Jasmine Johnson and her mother, who had returned without her son and was in a particularly bad mood. On my way back to my rental car I noticed someone across the street on a bicycle racing past the house and turning right onto one of the cross streets. In the glow of a dim streetlight, I caught a glimpse of red hair flowing from beneath the helmet; the rider was Jimmy Tucker, probably on his way home from the zoo and apparently in a hurry. He was riding one-handed, carrying a large paper bag in the other. I decided to follow him.

The streetlights became sparser as we headed west on Myrtle Lane, and eventually there were no lights. Jimmy had reached the outskirts of town and was heading into an unlit and unpopulated area. Fearing my headlights might make him suspicious, I pulled over and parked the car. I had lost sight of the boy now, but I followed on foot down the dark street as it narrowed into a dirt bike path.

The moon wavered behind gathering clouds as I entered a deeper forest. All was silent until an owl hooted, then departed in a rush from its high perch, gliding acrobatically through the tall trees and into the deepening blackness.

Ahead I could see the soft, golden glow of a single light, perhaps a quarter mile ahead. I followed along the rough hiking path that seemed to head directly toward the light. Suddenly I was jolted violently and thrown back off the path and into the tangled, thorny undergrowth. I must have lost consciousness for some time, for when I awoke, the moon had crested the forest and drifted toward a horizon I could not see. By the little flashlight on my key fob, I discovered that I had walked into the wire cables of a powerful electric fence.

Walking along the edge of the fence in search of an opening, I felt something hollow beneath my feet. Crouching there and digging with my hands, I uncovered a rectangular wooden frame, like a makeshift stretcher, camouflaged with leaves and branches. Pulling it up and away from the fence, I could see a short, narrow ditch leading down to a tunnel at the bottom. I slid down the ditch and followed through the tunnel to the other side. There was a wooden door there with an open padlock on it, leading upward and out of the tunnel. In his haste to get home, Jimmy Tucker must have neglected to lock the door. I was now entering the heart of a very old forest.

I had walked only a few yards toward the gold light when I tripped over some limp, bulky object. My flashlight revealed the half-eaten carcass of a large racoon. It was then that I sensed something else directly behind me.

Dreadfully, I turned to face two small lights, like glints of fire inside a black furnace. Staring at me was a giant cat crouched low on the path.

VI

In those moments when one's life seems about to end, there is a strangely familiar lucidity. It's as if one finds oneself in a theater where the stage has suddenly gone dark and silent, and there is a recognition of one's true self as a mere actor whose gig is suddenly up; the audience, the fellow actors, and even the props have all gone away. There is nothing but the soon-to-be former self looking into the eyes of imminent death. Yet ironically, what I heard in that moment was not the primal yawp of the Beast, but rather a deep and vibrant purring.

"Loco!" a voice called out. From the light ahead came running the red-haired boy. "Loco! It's OK. Time for supper."

A startled Jimmy Tucker recognized me right away. "Mr. James. Oh my... I had a feeling that...I know what you must be thinking, but please, you've got to let us explain."

With the great cat following along, sometimes like a faithful dog, other times like a giddy clown leaping from tree to tree, Jimmy led me toward the gold light, which emanated from a large cabin built upon the branches of three great oaks. We climbed a spiral staircase to the deck area (the cat preferring to use the tree trunk and branches) where we were greeted by an older black man with silver hair who sat drinking a beer. "Well, looky here, Jimmy. What did you find in the woods today?"

"Uncle Pete," replied Jimmy, "This is inspector James. He's here investigating the missing cougar."

"Well, then I guess the cat's out of the bag!" Uncle Pete exclaimed. It was hard to tell at the time whether he was laughing or crying, and I discerned a sadness in the old man there drinking beer in the dim light of an oil lantern. He seemed very tired. "Would you like to come inside—getting kind of chilly isn't it? Can I offer you a beer, or even a bit of moonshine if you promise not to tell?"

Considering the recent chain of incredible events, I accepted both offers and entered the surprisingly spacious home. Out on the deck I could hear the cat purring and growling simultaneously as it ate from a large bowl. From a separate room came sounds of gentle snoring. "That's little Tommy," said Uncle Pete, pouring me a small glass of some crystal-clear liquid and settling back in his rocking chair. "He's had a long day. And now I have a long story to tell you."

I learned that Peter White graduated with honors from Bucknell University in 1980, and was touted as just the seventh African American to ever graduate from its prestigious veterinary college. Soon after, he returned to Erie and set up a practice near the zoo. Later that year he married his secret high school sweetheart, Priscilla Campbell. Priscilla was a Scottish Catholic girl, whose parents would not have approved her dating a black person. It would take a long time for them to accept the marriage.

A year later, Electric General anticipated a change in their transportation infrastructure and decided to put some of their outlying territory up for sale. Peter bought fifty acres of old forest for cheap. He fenced the property in, and later applied the electric barrier. This was the beginning of the realization of a dream he and Priscilla had nurtured since high school: they began to design their own private research facility and nature preserve for rare and endangered species. However, a few years later, during the especially harsh winter of 1986, Priscilla fell ill with pneumonia. She died from fluid in the lungs in March.

Peter was a widower at 30 years old, and it was clear he never fully recovered from his heartbreak. He gave up on the nature preserve along with his private practice, and then went to work for the zoo, where he lasted 30 years, until a couple years ago when he ran into problems with Head Keeper Comden.

When funding was reduced by the state, Comden opted to cut costs from the direct care crew and not from the bloated salaries of the specialists. After several shouting matches with Comden, Dr. Peter White was demoted to night shift "management" duties. He was fired soon after for allegedly drinking on the job; one of the behaviorists found an empty beer bottle in the trash can outside the monkey complex. Hence, his retirement and retreat to the forest.

The boys were great-nephews of Peter White—the grandchildren of his sister. The boy's mother had endured an abusive relationship with the boys' father. Eventually, the parents split. Soon after, their mother married another man, who took a job in Pittsburgh and moved the family there. Unfortunately, he took little interest in the boys.

Jimmy became rebellious and spiteful. Tommy, who was afflicted with Albinism along with a speech impediment, had difficulty coping in a normal public-school environment. After numerous episodes with school officials and police, their mother decided she couldn't take it anymore. The boys had always been very fond of Uncle Pete, and at their mother's urgent behest, Dr. Peter White adopted them and brought them to the forest just a few years ago.

Moreover, I learned that Jimmy Tucker was not the only person in the cat complex the night Bellatrix was born. His little brother Tommy had a habit of sneaking away at night to keep Jimmy company. He would ride his bike to the zoo and enter through a small gap in the steel fencing that surrounded the facilities. On that night, Uncle Pete woke up to discover Tommy was missing. Knowing how close the brothers were, the doctor guessed where Tommy had gone. He drove to the zoo, parked on a back street, and used a copy of his old key to enter through the maintenance door. He was there in the cat house when the cubs were born.

Most significant was the news that there were actually *four* cubs in Medusa's litter, not three as Head-keeper Comden had told me. There was the stillborn, and there were the two females—the one sold to the Buffalo Zoo, and Bellatrix. The fourth kit was a male, and the mother was especially abusive toward him. The doctor determined that the male cub was in danger and they needed to get him away from the mother right away. While Jimmy distracted Medusa with a long stick, Doctor White entered the cage. When Bellatrix realized what was happening, she lunged at the doctor. But she was too late, and he escaped with the cub.

So they took him away as a newborn lion cub whose eyes were barely open. No one else would know, until now, that Loco even existed. It was here in the barn behind the treehouse that Uncle Pete and his nephews nourished and, as much as possible, trained the playful young cougar. At seven weeks, Dr. White anesthetized and neutered him, with slim hopes that he would remain docile long enough to formulate a plan for his future.

"So that's my story," sighed Uncle Pete, pouring himself another shot of moonshine. "That night was the last time I set foot in that zoo. And on the night of the escape last month, Jimmy was here with me. We did not let that cat out."

There was a long silence as Dr. White finished his story. Then he asked if I'd like to formally meet Loco, which was another offer I couldn't refuse. He opened the door and called for the cat, who after a few seconds entered leisurely. The animal was magnificent—over seven feet long from head to tail and weighing at least 130 pounds. Aside from the black spots that remained on his young head, he was cloaked in thick, tawny brown fur from his haunches to his powerful shoulders. His eyes, like fiery diamonds, looked curiously at me before he gently took a Milk bone from Uncle Pete. Then he was gone, back out into the night.

Suddenly, we heard in the distance the sound of several gunshots. "Things are getting pretty crazy around here, Mr. James," said Uncle Pete. "Lots of fools with guns these days. No doubt there's trouble ahead."

He continued. "So, Mr. James, what shall we do about all this? I suppose you'll need to write some kind of report about our little family here in the woods"

After some thought, I told him that as far as I was concerned, there is nothing here to report regarding the escaped cougar. But I gave him my cell phone number in case he heard anything.

With a sigh of relief, he replied, "Thank you sir. Though I don't think this will be our last meeting, do you? And I was thinking, perhaps you'd like to spend the night here on the couch, as opposed to making that nasty trek through the woods in the middle of the night after drinking some of this potion of mine? There might be wild animals out there!"

Here was one more offer I chose not to refuse. Uncle Pete brought me some blankets and retired to his room. As I lay back on the couch, amazed at the day's events, I could hear a gentle duet of the sleeping boys' breathing in the far room, interrupted by stuttered bursts of snoring from the good doctor. Somewhere in the woods, the great immature cat kept vigil while I dreamed of stars like raining spears through the night.

VII

In the morning Jimmy accompanied me back down the path and through the fence to the outside world. On my phone in the car were two messages. The first was from the agency, a firm reminder about how I must continue with the original plan. The second was from the Erie Police Chief informing me that we need to meet ASAP: there was trouble brewing in Bainesville.

I arrived at the Bainesville precinct to find a small army of officers. There had been an exchange of gunfire last night between a local gang and a platoon of white "hunters" from Pleasantville.

"It happened before midnight along the tracks that run from Bainseville to Pleasantville, at the border of Big Don Danforth's land," explained the chief. "A hunter was shot in the shoulder by one of the gang members. He's in stable condition and will survive, but Big Don, who owns the property where it all went down, is smoking mad…"

Just then a pickup truck came roaring up the driveway. A huge man—at least six feet six inches tall and well over 300 pounds—strode up to the chief, followed by a smaller fellow with darting, button eyes.

"I'm telling you Chief right now," hollered Big Don, "if you don't keep them bastards away from my land, there's gonna be a war! And if you or your men get in the middle of it out there, I aint accountable for your safety, cuz who knows which direction the bullets will be coming from. It's time to put up the damn wall, all across the border, and I aint paying for it. That's the county's job to keep them sons-o-bitches where they belong"

Big Don stormed out, followed by his partner with the mischievous eyes, and sped down the road. The chief then set the agenda: there would be three units of three officers each stationed at various locations along the tracks near the border until dark. Anyone with a gun and no license would be arrested immediately. Regarding the shooting, investigators already had a lead on a person of interest. A rival gang member had identified a Robert Johnson, of the *Da Vinci* gang, as the one who shot the hunter. Robert, Jade Johnson's big brother, was on the lam.

The day progressed with no further incidents. There was an apparent détente as the hunters returned to their houses and the gangs to their quads. There were, however, several anonymous threats of "Anglo-retaliation" called in and aired by local TV stations. In that uneasy truce, I drove back to the Johnson home.

Ms. Johnson's mood had changed, and this time she was anxious to see me. Robert had been gone for two days, and the local police had been cruising the street all day. She invited me to sit down in the living room. Breaking the awkward silence, I asked her about the paintings.

"Oh, those are Robert's. He was always so emotionally far-away as a child. But when something got hold of him, some idea or vision, he clung to it like a dog with a bone. When he got to painting, or writing, or reading about something, you couldn't break him away from it. You see, that locomotive picture—he loved trains as a boy. When they studied the history of the railroads at school, he just couldn't get enough of it. That was when we lived in the city, and he'd stay up at night just to hear them rumble down the tracks behind the house, coming in and then heading out, blowing that whistle...

"I think he loved the idea that people built these rails and these locomotives so that they could have the means to get away, move on, start something new in a brand-new place, you know, live the American dream..." She stopped short, suddenly aware that she was talking so much. "Anyway," she continued, "he was a beautiful young dreamer as a child, and, you know, with no regular father he had plenty of time to dream. Don't get me wrong—his father was not a bad man—but we were so young and so not ready. Before he got cancer, he would come around once every week or two to take Robby fishing out on the lake in this little boat he had..."

She paused, wiping away the tears that had started to fall. "And now Robby has taken up with some local gang. They call themselves Da Vinci's, probably my son's idea. But I have no clue as to what they do or where they go."

She shifted her gaze to the other painting, which I recognized as something similar to the scene I witnessed on my drive here yesterday. His version of the Lake Erie sunset, however, featured a small, dark fishing boat near the horizon. In the sky above the little boat was the image of a large, dreamlike sailboat that seemed to hover above the water like a great bird—its bow appeared as the head of an osprey, the stern spread like tail feathers, and the two unstayed masts were like great white wings.

"Now that one is a real mystery, isn't it?" said Jade Johnson. "I have no idea how he comes up with these ideas. But tell me, Mr. James. What kind of trouble is Robby in now?"

I assured her that the white man who was shot by the tracks was not critically wounded and he would recover, and that it would be difficult to prove who fired the gun. We talked for a long time as the night wore on and I explained to her that I knew people, good people, who could help Robert get on a better path in life, and that she should have a suitcase packed for him just in case there came a time when we needed to get him away from here quickly for his own protection.

Despite this ominous warning, Ms. Johnson seemed relieved and thanked me heartily as I left. The sun was setting again on my ride back to the hotel. Dark red and violet clouds hung like a plush canopy over Bainesville, casting the entire town in an eerie glow.

Most of the following day involved futile negotiations among police, gang leaders, and some folks from Pleasantville. It was clear that the different gang leaders had become tenuously united due to a common enemy. However, a common enemy does not always make for friendship or cooperation. There were several conflicting accounts from witnesses regarding the shooting, but it became clear that the main suspect was Robert Johnson.

On my way back to the hotel I received an urgent call from Dr. White: Little Tommy Tucker had disappeared. He was deeply concerned, given all the guns that were out there in the hundreds of acres of wilderness adjacent to his forest.

VIII

An hour later, I met Dr. White at the ditch by the fence where I had entered three nights ago. He had locked Loco in the cage in the barn, fearing that he would follow as we breached the borders of the forest in search of Tommy. "Loco is getting smarter every day, and more curious about the world," said Uncle Pete. "And you know what curiosity does to the cat!"

Following a deer path, first west and then south, Dr. White stopped abruptly at the edge of a ditch, smaller but similar to the one at the front entrance. We climbed down and through the tunnel, where he unlocked the small door leading up and out to the other side.

There the great forest abruptly diminished to a sparser growth of mixed vegetation— sumacs, locusts, silver maples mixed with young evergreens. The undergrowth was a dense, tangled mass of black raspberry thorn bushes, wild grape vines, and ivy. Whatever paths the doctor had made here had long surrendered to wild growth. There were no signs of Tommy, so we returned to the forest, then proceeded north to the next exit.

It was nearly dark when we passed through that tunnel to the adjacent property. There we discovered a narrow path leading into a stand of tall evergreens. It was so quiet, so tranquil inside those woods. At that moment it occurred to me that if this was the trail Tommy had taken, he was headed in the direction of the recently militarized zone near Big Don's property.

Suddenly a shot rang out. I sprinted ahead of the doctor up the path toward where it opened into a field. Twenty yards away I saw a young dark-skinned man, or boy, with his hand on the throat of Tommy Tucker. "You stupid kid...I should have shot both of you!" he was shaking Tommy like a doll.

"Robert! Stop!" I yelled. He swung around, pointing a pistol at me.

"I talked with your mother. She's worried sick about you. Now listen, believe me, we can fix this. But right now we need to get away from here. The wrong people must have heard that shot, and they will come. Let Tommy go and come with us"

Reluctantly, Robert complied, and the two boys followed back down the path, where we met an out-of-breath Doctor Pete. "We've got to get out of here fast," he gasped.

It was dark by the time we made it back to Dr. White's treehouse. Surprisingly, Robert and Jimmy knew each other from school, and had been friends up until Robert got involved with the gangs. Robert explained that he was in those woods not to shoot at the hunters, but rather to hunt down the animal that had nearly killed his sister. His mother, he told us, worked hard but had bills she was barely able to pay. The $2000.00 would help with the medical bills and Christmas presents for his sister. It was his right to kill that animal.

Robert had the cougar in his sights. It was standing still in plain sight across the field at the edge of the spruce woods, a perfect shot. But just as he was ready to fire, Tommy came running out of the trees in front of the cat. At the last split second, Robert shifted his aim and shot wide into the air. He narrowly avoided what would have been a terrible tragedy.

The five of us—Doc, Jimmy, Tommy, Robert, and I, sat silently for some time. Then the doctor sighed, much troubled by all this. "Tommy, what were you doing out there today? You know I have told you over and over again never to leave this property without Jimmy or me with you, especially after you found that girl last month. Boy, you could have been killed!"

Then Tommy spoke up, nearly crying with frustration. "It's not fair," he stuttered. "Jimmy has Loco. I want a cougar too. I could take good care of her, but now she won't let me. I used to feed her at the zoo, and she liked me better than the rest. She never growled at me. But now she runs away every time I try to give her Milk bones!"

Uncle Pete knelt beside the boy. "Tommy, did you let Bellatrix out of her cage at the zoo? How in the world were you able to…"

"It's my fault," said Jimmy. "I should have known. I taught Tommy how to sneak into the zoo, and I had a feeling he was going there even when I wasn't working. And I knew how much he loved Bellatrix. But I had no idea he would let her go."

So it was Tommy who had doused the lights near Bellatrix' cage and the zoo's exit gate. He'd used a key he stole from Uncle Pete to unlatch the cage; then, with sandwich meat, he coaxed her to the hole in the fence and out of the zoo. But once he was on his bike, Bellatrix followed only for the first hundred yards. Then she went rogue, running away from the road and into the woods. Tommy had been looking for her ever since. He'd been skipping school for a month, but the attendance office had never bothered to contact Uncle Pete.

As for Robert, he was a wanted man, and in danger from all fronts—the white hunters, the police, and a rival gang that set him up to look like the shooter near Big Don's property. We decided the safest place for him right now was here with Uncle Pete.

It was nearly midnight when I arrived at Jade Johnson's home. She was relieved to know that Robert was safe, but deeply concerned about his future. I reassured her that I knew people who could help, but that she must be ready and willing to let him go far away from here. With a sigh of resignation, Jade offered me a glass of wine. We drank and talked into the wee hours as I tried to explain all the crazy things that had happened. At length, she insisted I get some sleep on her couch, an offer I accepted gratefully.

I was awakened from a pleasant dream by a message from *The Tower*: *A large package has been sent to your hotel. You'll need to rent a van. You'll also need someone, maybe more than one person, to help you, people you can trust. Oh, and you'll need a live rabbit.*

IX

Early the next morning I exchanged my rental car for a van. By the time I returned, there was a package outside the hotel the size of a freezer but remarkably light in weight. I loaded it into the van and found a pet store where I purchased an adult male rabbit, white as snow. That evening I drove straight to Dr. White's preserve, entered through the front ditch, and found him and Tommy in the barn working on a scale model of his property. Loco lay quietly in a cage. He yawned and twitched his tail as I entered.

"Hello Inspector James. We meet again so soon. Tommy and I are playing with some ideas about a little zoo of our own."

The doctor informed me that Jimmy and Robert were exploring the woods. He also explained that Loco had been up to some mischief lately and needed to be caged for the time being. Since he turned a year old, his wanderlust was getting the better of him. It would be necessary to keep a closer eye on him as he matured.

I told the doctor about my orders to catch Bellatrix alive. First, I needed to get the vehicle onto his property and unload the package. He agreed, and within a half hour he had shut down the electricity and rolled the fence back enabling me to pull in far enough to be out of sight from the dirt road.

The package contained what appeared to be some kind of cage, one made from transparent, glass-like cables, nearly invisible. There were two handles on the top, and as I pulled on them, the cage expanded, and a trap door appeared on top of the front side. Inside, at the back end, there was a much smaller cage made of the same material. Above it was a curious device that looked like a radio; I pushed a button and a strange mixture of sounds and scents emanated from it—soothing strings and various animal calls blended with a pungent aroma I could not identify. Loco sat up in his cage instantly, highly intrigued by the sound. I shut it off.

"I have heard about these new traps," said Dr. White. "State of the art, if trapping animals can be considered an art."

We determined the best time and place to set the trap would be after dark in the area outside the evergreen forest where Robert had nearly shot Tommy. That evening at dusk Jimmy and I dragged the trap down the path through the ditch and out into the evergreen woods. Tommy carried the sacrificial rabbit (which we assured him would not be harmed) and Dr. White brought his old-school veterinarian medical bag, which contained, among other tools of the trade, the gun he would use to tranquilize the cat once we had trapped it.

I turned on the radio, set the trap door, and placed the bunny inside the small cage. The soft drone of strange music filled the silence as we waited anxiously by the tunnel door, which we had left unlatched to expedite the transport back to the house after we trapped Bellatrix.

It was a warm and clear October night as we sat there at the edge of the field, waiting and watching for a lion in the woods. The height of the season of comets and meteorites was past. However, as the night wore on, I spotted several stars shoot across the sky like fiery spears.

Suddenly, in a violent rush from behind, we were ambushed by a powerful figure, one that raced right on past us! We realized then that Loco had escaped from his cage was now heading to the trap!

As we scrambled to follow him, there was a sudden unearthly scream, then another. And then there was a savage exchange of hissing, growling, and yowling. As we came to the trap, we saw Loco and Bellatrix tangled together in primordial battle. Bellatrix, though smaller, was the fiercer of the two, but Loco defended himself, and would not retreat.

Then there was the muffled sound of a shot, followed by another. Dr. White had managed to shoot Loco with a tranquilizer dart, and then Bellatrix as she tried to run away. Both beasts reeled in circles as if drunk, then slumped to the ground. Within a minute they were motionless.

Now with two doped cougars and one empty cage, we scrambled to recover. "Hurry!" cried the Doctor. "We're going to have an audience soon." After removing the small rabbit cage from the large one, Jimmy dragged Bellatrix's limp body to the cage and managed to shove her inside. Dr. White instructed Robert to run and bring back the thatched ditch cover by the tunnel door, which we would use as a sled/stretcher to transport Loco. Soon both mountain lions were secured, and we began to drag them toward the tunnel, Bellatrix first. I managed to get her and her cage through to safety on the other side while Jimmy and the doctor struggled behind getting Loco onto the stretcher.

Jimmy was dragging Loco toward the tunnel when we were suddenly aware of a shifting beam from a flashlight across our path. Then a huge figure—a mountain of a man wearing camouflage hunting attire—emerged from the evergreens, his rifle pointed straight at us. Jimmy, Dr. White, and I froze. The giant was then joined by another smaller hunter with a rifle.

"Drop what you're doing right now!" said Big Don. "What's goin on here? What the hell???…" He stared incredulously at Loco's limp body, and then at Uncle Pete. Well, will you look at this, Johnny. It's the Witch Doctor, all the way from Africa, poaching on my property."

"Yeah, Donny," laughed the smaller man, whose little button eyes darted every which way. "Must be Dr. Doolittle is out on a safari."

"That cat there is on my property," said big Don. "That means he's mine, and so is that $2000.00 reward. What do you say, Johnny?" Johnny smiled, flashing single-digit teeth.

The next moment, a dark figure came speeding out from the woods straight at Big Don, knocking away the rifle and tackling him to the ground, then raining down blows to his head. Johnny was startled. He aimed his gun but couldn't take the chance of shooting his partner. Instead, he jumped on top of the attacker, striking at him with his rifle stock.

Then Jimmy rushed in, taking Johnny down, and there was a full-fledged brawl happening at the woods' edge. Dr. White shouted to me, "Take Tommy and the cats now. Get them out of here!"

I managed to drag Loco through the tunnel and lift him on top of the cage. Then I mounted the cage on top of the thatch cover. Using it as a sled, we began pulling both pumas down the path toward the barn. A minute later I heard a gunshot. Fearing the worst, I lunged forward in a last-ditch effort to get the cougars back to the treehouse.

Ten minutes minutes later, as Tommy and I arrived back at the house, Jimmy and Robert caught up. They were breathless, their clothes ripped from the fight. Jimmy gasped, "The gun went off. Someone was shot—I think it was the big one. Uncle Pete is helping him. He told me to tell you to send supplies. He said you would know what to do."

I went to the barn and gathered up emergency flares, a gallon jug of water, a large lighter, and a jug of moonshine, and a jackknife. Placing it all in a wheelbarrow, I told Jimmy to take Tommy. Robert was going with me.

From the van, I called 911 and told them of the emergency in the woods near the tracks between Bainesville and Pleasantville. They would need a helicopter to get there. I knew it would be at least an hour before they found where Big Don had been shot. That would give me enough of a head start to get back to Jade's house, and then to contact the Tower to receive my final instructions regarding delivery of not one, but two cougars. Hopefully, the big cats would not wake up before the rendezvous.

I took Loco's cage from the barn and placed it at the edge of the van, securing the latch he had broken in his escape with heavy wire. I then hoisted man-sized mass of limp lion and shoved him inside. Next, I hoisted Bellatrix' trap, then pushed both cages forward toward the front seats and closed the rear doors. The doctor had left the electricity to the fence shut off, and I was able to roll back enough of it to pull the van out onto the dirt road.

It was after midnight when we arrived back at Robert's home. Jade Johnson was waiting for us. Beside her on the floor was a large suitcase packed with Robert's belongings, along with an envelope containing a letter. After tending to Robert's wounds—mostly just scratches from the thorns during the fight, she shoved the letter into his hand. "Read this once you have arrived safely," she said firmly. "Now you must go with Mr. James."

X

I learned later that the medics did arrive at the scene by helicopter and that Big Don took a bullet from his own gun to his right arm. Dr. White had disinfected it (with moonshine!) and covered the wound before the emergency crew took over. Big Don survived, but he would have little use of that arm for the rest of his life.

Afterwards, the news reporters struggled to fashion a plausible story as to the cause of the shooting. Big Don and Johnny were close-lipped about the whole event, fearing that no one would believe their story about not one, but two dead cougars. They had no evidence, and it seemed in their best interest to let sleeping cats lie, so to speak. They would stick with the more believable story of being jumped in the woods by gang members. They were promised a full investigation, but as time went on, Big Don decided to drop the case.

I also learned later about Dr. White's clever ruse to put the fugitive mountain lion story to rest. He had a long-time friend, a Mr. Green, who was not only the head of the local branch of the Erie County Animal Control Agency, but also a taxidermist. He happened to have a full-grown cougar preserved in a crouching position, as if preparing to strike. It was not a piece of work Mr. Green was especially proud of, and he was willing to sacrifice it for the greater good. By applying a quantity of blood (to which he had considerable access given his day job) to the stuffed lion's body, along with a few last-minute limb contortions, he was able to produce a puma that appeared to have been hit by a car.

The good doctor took credit for this last act—the unfortunate accident that dented his front bumper. The taxidermist was first on the scene, covering the beast in a bloody blanket and loading it into the service truck. The police chief, much relieved to have heard this news, arrived promptly, and after taking photographs of the fake lion, he instructed Mr. Green to either dispose of it or keep it for stuffing. Later that day, with only a trace of regret, Mr. Green saw to it personally that the fabled beast was reduced to ashes at the county incinerator. The reward money was donated to the local SPCA.

One more detail: Tommy recovered the white rabbit and took it safely back home to the barn.

XI

At the farthest eastern reaches of Presque Isle there will be a light due north. Flash three times and wait. This was the last message from the agency, which came as I turned onto Lake Shore Drive heading back to Erie. It was the wee hours of the morning.

Presque Isle during October is a quiet place, all but deserted after the tourist season. The ghosts of another harsh winter-to-come were already stirring when we entered the State Park. As I pulled off the road onto the northernmost beach of the peninsula, wind driven waves charged the shore, their white knuckled hands clamoring, one after another, higher up the beach, snatching sand and stones back in the undertow. It was hard to imagine that, across these unfathomable, dark waters and no more than 70 miles away, was Canada.

There were stirrings now in the back of the van, and one of the cats let out a pathetic moan. Time was of the essence.

I positioned the van to face due north and flashed my headlights three times. Shortly after, a single gold light appeared in the distance. There was no moon above, and the constellations were brilliant. Orion was directly above us, with Cassiopeia settling just above the western horizon. Then I witnessed something incredible: the sky filled suddenly with a dozen shooting stars all at once, like a stream of gleaming arrows across the sky.

The wind calmed with the arrival of the ship—a large cabin cruiser named *Gaia*. Robert was surprised to see two beautiful young female crew members, one Asian, the other African, dressed in emerald green uniforms with gold trim. Their mission was clear: get the cougar aboard, keep it moderately sedated, and deliver it to its final destination, as directed by the Tower.

They were surprised, of course, to learn of the second cougar. But when I told them about the boy, they looked very confused and anxious. The Asian woman went below to make a call. After a minute, she returned, motioning for the boy to board the vessel. For the first time, Robert looked directly at me, his eyes filled with sadness and resignation. I assured him that he would be with his mother and sister again someday soon.

Dawn broke as the *Gaia* returned to the high waters. As I watched her fade into the morning light, it seemed she could have been a mere fishing boat now, a dark speck, perhaps ready to be reborn into a sailboat, and then a great bird that would rise, taking flight above the gold, shimmering waters.

The High Jumper

I

He lay in the creek between two large rocks, his body motionless amid the swirling and frothing of sticks and plastic bottles. There was no blood, no sign of foul play—just the body of an older Caucasian male in a plain brown jacket, underdressed for the mid-April Colorado weather. This had been a tall man, well over six feet. Most peculiar were his deformed hands—three fingers on each, webbed near the knuckles, tapering to claw-like tips. He lay in the water face down, the back of his jacket billowing atop the swirling spring current.

Crouching down into the stream, I managed to get enough leverage to grip him beneath his arm pits and pull him up and onto the sand bar. As I turned him face up, it appeared that the bloating had dulled his features, as if the man had left the body long ago. I imagined him to be about sixty years old, well-built despite apparent malnutrition, and judging by his over-worn boots, much traveled. I searched his pockets for ID, finding nothing but a key chain fob engraved with an image of Pike's Peak and a bookmarker with a St. Jude prayer on it issued by St. Mary's Church.

I waited there contemplating the dead man as the afternoon sun warmed the creek bed and clumps of snow fell like over-ripe fruit from the trees lining Memorial Park. Joggers paused and gawked from the trail above. From the power lines spanning the opposite banks of the creek, a choir of pigeons scattered away as the ambulance arrived. Soon after came the coroners, who seemed unaffected by the image in front of them

"Third one this month" said the first.

"Yeah, my ex-wife always told me this is a dead end job" joked the other as they began to position him for transport. I left them with the requisite indignities of their occupation.

St. Mary's Church, well known for its charity toward the homeless, was just upstream from the bridge where the man had been found. I was able to speak with one of the priests, along with several volunteers, who told me that their mission helps hundreds of homeless people every week, providing meals, counseling, and recommendations for the local shelters. I described the tall man with the deformed fingers, but no one seemed to recall him specifically. However, one parishioner informed me of a camp downstream. A small community, maybe ten homeless adults, had formed there at the bottom of two steep banks. The only access to it was a walking trail along the creek, which was especially hard during the spring currents. The police had largely ignored the camp despite public complaints about the heaps of trash visible from the homes atop the cliffs.

I set out that afternoon on a crude path of sand bars, exposed tree roots, and flat rocks. After about a mile of stilted travel along the swift-running creek (and having thoroughly soaked both my shoes) I arrived at the camp. It consisted of several plastic tarps cleverly draped and fastened among a stand of young poplars at the bottom of two sheer cliffs. As I approached, a grey-haired, leather-faced woman peered at me suspiciously from behind a flap. Excusing myself and holding out the bookmark and the keychain, I asked her if she knew the owner. As she glanced at the items, her eyes darted away, as if she had seen something fly across the stream. She stared blankly into that space for some time, then uttered almost imperceptibly, "Hermie". There would be no last name offered, only a long silence.

"Wait" she said at last as I turned to leave. The old woman limped over to a shopping cart full of god-knows-what and began to dig through its contents. She returned shortly, handing me an oversized plastic bar soap container, the contents of which made it feel heavy. Waving me off, she disappeared within the tent. As I turned and began the trudge back upstream, I could hear the muffled sounds of sobbing or laughing, I could not tell which. A short time later, I heard a piercing wail, an un-earthly sound. At the same moment a great blue heron flew up from a cove on the opposite bank, careened around a bend and disappeared.

It was dusk by the time I returned to the park. To the west, the Rocky Mountains hulked like massive shadows beneath a fading red glow, the embers of the day. As I stood on the bridge, a pair of ducks paddled dreamily in the stream below where the body had lain. There, under the pale-yellow street-light, I opened the soap dish.

Inside was an old car key—from a Chevy, a 60's or 70's model I guessed. There also was a silver pendant with an etching of an American eagle. Beneath those items were two faded photographs. The first was a close-up of a young girl with dark red hair, drifting eyes, and a mouth that seemed to smile sadly. The other picture was much older—a black and white shot of a man in a US Airforce uniform posing by a picnic table in some park. His expression seemed to convey a bold and daring character.

Most interesting and perhaps useful was a 2nd place ribbon from a high jump competition at the New York State high school track meet finals in 1972. Under the ribbon was a folded piece of paper. It was a page ripped out of a book with a disturbing poem called "Eating the Birds" by Margaret Atwood. Highlighted were these lines…*we wanted their wings / we wanted to fly as they did / soar freely among the treetops and the clouds / and so we ate them.*

The last item was the most beautiful and unusual miniature snow globe I had ever seen. It was egg-shaped, but flat on the bottom. Its glass exterior served as a protective shell for the figure inside—a brilliant red heart in the center of a pair of emerald wings. As I turned it in my hand toward the light, the wings flapped gracefully through a gentle snowfall.

Later in my room at the Antlers Hotel, I tried to contact the Tower. However, it was becoming more and more evident that I was largely on my own with these investigations. The agency seemed aloof, despite having assured me of their support in times of need.

I decided to take another look at the contents of the soap dish. There, crumpled in a ball in the corner was a gum wrapper. I opened it to discover what appeared to be a ten-digit phone number, the area code from somewhere upstate New York.

It was already past ten o'clock in New York, but I decided to try the number anyway. The first two times, the call was cut off. On the third try, someone answered, her voice seemed very guarded, very reluctant to talk. I explained briefly why I was calling, after which she replied coldly, "Please do not dig up old graves" and hung up.

II

The next day, I tried to have the number traced, but it turned out to be a disposable phone, one that had been purchased years ago. However, I was able to discover the results of the New York State championship high jump competition of 1972, which identified a Connor Larson, from Seneca Hill High School in upstate New York, as the second-place finisher that year. More research revealed that Larson had died in 1978 in a climbing accident on Mount Marcy, the highest peak in the Adirondacks.

Through the class reunion website, I was able to contact several classmates. I got pretty much the same story from all of them: Connor was a recluse, a loner, a "closed book," most likely due to his birth defect which some of them referred to as "claw hands". I was referred by one of his mates on the track team to their coach and English teacher, Mr. Thomas, who was always very protective of Connor. I learned that Mr. Thomas, already several years into retirement, resided now at the Norfolk Home in Oswego, NY. The question now loomed: if this was Connor Larson, then who died back in 1978 on Mount Marcy?

The next morning, I was on a plane to Syracuse, NY.

III

I arrived in Syracuse that evening to a foot-deep carpet of late April snowfall, upon which the plane had made a rough landing. I decided to stay in the city that evening and drive to Oswego the next day. After a barbeque dinner and a bottle of wine at a blues club called the Dinosaur Bar and Grill, I checked in at the Marriott across the street.

I awoke to a wild cacophony of birds singing in the hotel courtyard. Flocks of goldfinches had returned from their southern refuge, and the air breathed promise. It was a brilliant morning; the sun shone through a pure blue sky, buds were golden in the trees, and the snow was melting rapidly from the roof and splashing on the terrace. After breakfast in the cafe, I drove north toward Oswego.

The main lobby in The Norfolk Home featured a large window overlooking Lake Ontario. A short, heavy-set nurse greeted me at the desk. Leading me to Mr. Thomas' room, she forewarned me that he had been struggling lately with his speech, and that his attention span was very short. We arrived in a room with barren white walls and a single window facing a neighboring building across an alley. Sitting in a wheelchair was a frail, white-haired man in pajamas who appeared to be asleep. His knees rose above the level of the chair's arms as he slumped there, chin on chest, and it occurred to me he had been a very tall man in his youth. The nurse nudged him firmly, and at length he opened his eyes and lifted his chin slightly from his chest.

"Mr. Thomas, are you with us?" she hollered, overly articulating each syllable. "Inspector James is here to visit with you. He has some questions to ask."

The man tried to focus his gaze upon me as I sat down in a chair across from him. I began by asking about his days working at Seneca Hill High School. He seemed to brighten for a moment, as if struck by a fleeting recollection. Then he sighed, shifted in his seat and looked away, as if he'd forgotten I was there. But when I spoke the name Connor Larson, he seemed startled and returned his attention to me.

"Mr. Thomas," I continued. "I am concerned about Connor. I have belongings of his that may be of value to someone, and I have come to you as one who, I am told by his classmates, knew him well. I would like to find a home for these belongings." Mr. Thomas shifted again nervously. Then, with more clarity in his eyes, nodded for me to continue.

I removed the picture of the Airforce pilot from the soap box and showed it to him. Mr. Thomas appeared uncomfortable in its presence, and looked away to the floor, shaking his head. When I showed him the photograph of the girl, he paused, then smiled sadly. "Criteen" he uttered, closing his eyes, as if a pleasant dream had visited him. There was no response to the pendant or the car key, but when I showed the second-place ribbon from the high jump competition, he became very agitated, spitting out words I could not understand. I paused, waiting for him to calm down.

At length, I removed the globe and held it out to Mr. Thomas. In that moment, an expression of amazed lucidity lit upon his face, as if he had witnessed the rapture. A moment later, Mr. Thomas sat slumped forward, dead in his chair.

IV

I rushed to the nurses' station to report what had just happened. "Probably a heart attack," replied the plump one who had escorted me to his room. She seemed unconcerned. "He's been hanging by a thread for months."

It was clear to me how immune to the deaths of their temporary guests these nurses must become. I almost wished that they would accuse me of something, if only to have conveyed some measure of feeling. But no. It was just a day in the life for them, and the fact that it was the last day in the life of a patient was unremarkable at this point.

After driving back to my hotel room from my fateful visit with Mr. Thomas, I drank plenty of wine trying to ward off the dreams that had been stirring of late—voices calling me for help, but they are too far away, across a deep ravine. I am not sure whether I was in the dream or the real world when I heard my phone chime. *Paul,* whispered the voice of a woman or a girl, I could not distinguish which. *You are on the right path. Have faith.*

I returned to Oswego the following morning, intent on gleaning any scraps of information from the Norfolk Home regarding Mr. Thomas' family. It did not take long. Gathering Mr. Thomas' last possessions in his room was a tall, elegant, middle-aged woman with long auburn hair. She flashed discerning eyes over me as I stood in the doorway. "So, are you the one who caused my father's heart attack?" she said with a straight face. She then smiled sadly. "I'm kidding, of course, though I am curious as to why you are here."

She introduced herself as Christine Thomas, and I knew immediately that she was the young girl in the photograph. It was alarming how little she had changed over all the years, and how youthful and attractive she was now.

Perhaps that is partly why, after glancing at her ring-less left hand, I invited her to dinner that evening. At first she refused, but when I told her of the possessions in the soap container, she agreed to meet with me that evening after she had put all her father's affairs in order.

V

We met that warm spring evening at the Heron Nest Restaurant overlooking the Oswego River. She wore a tight fitting, dark green dress, her lovely long legs making it seem shorter than it really was. I hope you don't mind," she said, intercepting my clumsy double-take. "It's going to be black attire for the next few days."

"Anyway," she continued, "I am the one who received your call the other day, Mr. James. And I do still wish you would leave well enough alone. But we have come this far, and of course whenever one story ends, another begins. So, how can I help you?"

After dinner we sat for a long time at the table by the window overlooking the river. I learned that she was a physical therapist living and working in Syracuse. Her father's death was long expected, especially after he came down with pneumonia. He had had one foot on the other side for a while, she said, long enough to let it all finally go despite his stubborn nature.

Then Christine began to tell me the story of Connor Larson.

VI

"It is a sad story, Mr. James, one that began long before I was born.

"My father, Brian Thomas, and Connor's mother, Mary Fennel (from home), grew up on the same street in Seneca Hill. They had been close friends since childhood. By the time they were in high school, Brian, who was a year younger, had not matured as rapidly as some of the other boys. Mary who already was a beautiful young woman, always treated him like a little brother. She did not suspect how deeply he felt for her, but such is the way with teenagers, eh?

"My father, who had grown steadily taller and more athletic throughout high school, was heartbroken when, just after her high school graduation, Mary agreed to marry United States Airforce Airman Walter Larson, who was four years older than Mary and about to go off to the war in the Pacific.

For my father, life in Seneca Hill without Mary was meaningless, so he enlisted in the Marines. He served in France during and after the war. Finally, in 1950, he came back to the only home he knew, Seneca Hill, and tried to lead a normal life. He had studied physical education at Oswego State College, then became a teacher and a coach at the high school. He married my mother, Katherine, shortly thereafter.

"Walter Larson, meanwhile, had been promoted to captain after receiving a Medal of Honor. He retired after the war ended, planning to start a family with Mary. However, they had difficulty conceiving a child. It was assumed that this was Mary's fault, and the captain, despite Mary's misgivings, convinced her to receive fertility injections. It was part of the great American plan to increase the nation's post-war population. The drugs were experimental, of course, but it seemed to be in everyone's best interest, and for some, like Walter Larson, tantamount to patriotic duty.

"Captain Larson took a job flying for Trans-World Airlines, which paid very well. He then bought a fancy house on the outskirts of Seneca Hills. However, as a commercial pilot for an international company, the Captain was away most of the time. Mary, who despite having a college degree in education, was discouraged from working. Her job was to take care of the house, and, hopefully, bear Walter a child.

"When it became clear that Mary was pregnant a year later, Captain Larson was elated. After much self-congratulation, he promised to try to be home more often. However, it turned into a very difficult pregnancy for Mary. Morning sickness was more like all-day sickness, and her doctor was concerned about the fetus. Nevertheless, she managed to deliver a healthy boy, albeit one with a prominent birth defect—a deformity of the hands. Today it is referred as syndactyly; back then it was the stuff of freak shows. I've read recently there has been research suggesting a connection between fertility drugs and birth defects.

"And so the Larson marriage continued to unravel. Walter grew distant, unable to feel the pride and affection he had hoped for regarding his son, and apparently he felt a degree of repulsion when he looked at the hands of the boy. When Connor was just two years old, Walter claimed that the airline was relocating him to the west coast. Mary knew this was a lie—that he had requested the transfer—but she had lost what little love she ever had for him a long time ago. She would never see or hear from Walter Larson again. And whatever secrets she held within her sad and lonely heart would remain deeply hidden."

VII

After requesting another glass of wine, Christine continued. "As a child, Connor was very quiet. It was as if he had inherited his mother's timid nature. As a boy, whenever he asked her where his father was, she simply pointed to the sky: 'Up there. Fighting the enemy.' Connor determined at a very young age that he too would be able to fly someday. And I suppose in a way, he did.

"As a teenager, Connor was very athletic, despite his hands. He suffered from teasing and some bullying, but he learned to defend himself very well, and people left him alone for the most part. As he grew tall and strong, the coaches tried to get him to play football and basketball, but he chose only track and field, which my father coached. As you may know, Connor was a renowned high jumper—he still holds the state record. No one has come close.

"So you are probably wondering why only the second-place ribbon? According to my father, Connor could out-jump the boy who won by at least six inches. But for some reason, Connor threw the contest. He was missing at heights that had been easy for him, and as he approached the bar for his last jump, he abruptly stopped in front of the bar and knocked it off with his hand. Then he walked away. The next day, after the lonely ride home from the meet, he disappeared.

"His mother, Mary, would hear from him via postcard from time to time over the next five years, and he called home once. She was devastated, and she could never stop worrying about him. It turned out that he had been living in the Adirondacks, working odd jobs, and doing a lot of climbing, his deformed hands apparently not a handicap as he obsessed over the challenges of those mountains. According to another rock climber who knew Connor, there was a sheer cliff on the side of Mount Marcy that no one had ever dared to climb, but Connor had vowed to do it.

"He plummeted over a hundred feet, his fall partially broken by the branches of a tree in the gulley below. A group of hikers found him still breathing, who knows how many hours later. They called 911, and Connor was transported by Mercy flight to Syracuse General Hospital. After landing, they rushed him to the ER, where he was diagnosed as comatose. He was put on life support system and transferred to ICU.

Connor carried no identification on him, but a phone number was found in his pocket—that of his mother. A hospital staff member called right away, hoping to get information about the victim. As they described the young man over the phone, Mary panicked and hung up.

I had just arrived home from work at the Emergicare center across town from Syracuse General when I got the hysterical call from Mary. I left for the hospital immediately, still wearing my scrubs.

"The place was quiet and understaffed as I made my way to the intensive care unit. Inside were several curtained-off beds. There were six with patients on ventilators, but none of them was Connor. Then I saw one empty bed near the window, the sheets cast aside. I realized at that moment Connor must have regained consciousness and left on his own.

"My first reaction was to alert the nurse on duty, and to call the police to search the area. But just then something told me I must let him go. I knew he would resist attempts to be apprehended and forced back to the hospital. He would be like a bird in a cage. If he was well enough to walk, he would survive. And, in a way, he had already left this world, years ago.

"I went to the nurse's station, where just one nurse was on duty. She appeared half asleep as I approached. Probably because I was still in scrubs, she believed me when I told her that the comatose patient by the window had died and was sent to the morgue.

"Of course, there was mass confusion in the aftermath of that night, as no one could account for the whereabouts of the unidentified mountain climber. An investigation is still pending, complicated by the fact that I managed to get an obituary published in the *Seneca Hill Observer* after I convinced Connor's mother that he had died.

"I suppose I should feel a heavy burden of responsibility. But, on the other hand, I had managed to give Connor a head-start to wherever his journey would take him. And, more importantly, I was able to give his mother closure after all the years of being sick with worry about her only child.

"So you see, Mr. James, if it is a crime you are investigating here, well, you have found me out. But please, no handcuffs."

VIII

I assured her that I had no such intentions, but that I believed there was more to it than she had let on. "So what was your relationship with Connor?" I asked.

"Oh, we were friends, as were our parents. His mother, Mary, was like a second mother to me, and of course my father took great interest in him as an athlete and as a student. Connor was a few years older than me, and I had known him since I was a little girl. His deformity was never something I even thought about. Those were the hands of Connor Larson, and he was like a big brother to me. Later, as teenagers, we became very close, and would spend a great deal of time together..." She paused, staring out the window.

"He would drive me up here from Seneca Falls. Downriver, just a few miles from where we are sitting now, there was path leading through a small forest to a reservoir, a beautiful spot where we would spend hours just talking. It was so secluded; hardly anyone knew about it. And Connor was so thought-ful, so curious about life...You could see the trees from the opposite shore per-fectly reflected upside down in the shimmering water. Oh, and the birds – especially the herons! Over time, they were no longer startled by us when we came from the woods, but rather seemed to accept our presence as they waded in the shallows spearing for fish.

"Anyway, we were together a lot—more than what was healthy, according to my mother, Katherine, who suddenly, on my thirteenth birthday in June, forbade me from seeing Connor at all. And she made it clear to Connor's mother Mary that he was to stay away from me. I fought with my mother ter-ribly over that; for the next few months I was incorrigible, and there were sev-eral ugly episodes. Eventually, when it was clear that I was on a self-destructive path, my parents decided I should go away to a boarding school in Pough-keepsie to finish secondary school.

"It was not from my mother that I learned the truth. It was Mary who told me about her affair with my father during a time when Walter Larson was away. I barely understood what this meant, but I felt the gravity of it intensely. Suddenly the whole world seemed deformed, and Connor was a part, if not the cause, of that deformity. As I steeled myself, Connor fell apart, and after he learned what I had learned, he took to the mountains.

"I saw him only once more after high school. It was the summer of 2008, and there was a small group of homeless people hanging on the streets near my office in Syracuse. As I offered a dollar bill to this tall, dirty man, I saw the hand that I had known so well. He did not recognize me, or else he chose not to, I don't know which. But as he turned away, I yelled for him to wait. I grabbed a piece of gum from my purse, ripped off the wrapper, and wrote my phone number on it. I took his deformed hand, opened it, put the wrapper inside. Then I closed those three beloved fingers around it. I ran, knowing I would never see him again.

IX

After Christine had finished, I opened the soap container and placed each of the items on the table. She picked them up one by one.

"This key was to his 1961 Chevy Biscayne, his first and only car—the one we drove to the lake.

"This is a picture of Captain Larson right after WWII. And the medallion was a gift from him to Connor. Connor tried so hard to not judge him, and he always had his own dream of learning to fly…"

She took a long time reading the poem "Eating the Birds" by Margaret Atwood. "I've never seen this before. How terribly sad it is. But it makes sense in light of what he went through."

"The ribbon you know about. And my father, he never got over Connor quitting on that day in June. It was as if his own heart had been ripped out and thrown onto the cinders."

She sighed deeply as she took the snow globe in her hand, her jaw set firmly as if to hold back the tears. "This was a gift from my father to Mary, then from Mary to Connor, and later from Connor to me. Or, I should say, it is half a gift."

In the table's candlelight, she shook the egg gently and turned it over, the snow swirling gently. The red heart seemed to pulse in anticipation as the little emerald wings flapped softly. Then, setting it down, she reached into her purse and removed another, almost identical globe, this one with golden wings. As she placed it on the table next to the first, the two seemed to respond to each other—their hearts beating, their wings relentless in their quest to make their separate worlds one.

"May I keep this?" she asked, the tears running down her face freely now.

Of course she would keep the globe. Perhaps she had never really lost it. It had just been away for a long time, and now it had come home.

Battle of the Bands

Tipped off by an anonymous source, the police found him tied to a rusted old Ferris Wheel tub in a junkyard on the outskirts of town. It had been only a couple of hours, but he was shivering and breathing heavily, in a state of near panic. According to the report, he had been jumped from behind outside his home and forced face-first to the ground, where his head was covered with a burlap sack. He was then tied up at the wrists, muscled into the backseat of a big old car, and driven to the junkyard to be deposited there in a drizzling rain. Thus Mr. Bernard Bauer was prevented from being a judge in the 20th annual Battle of the Bands at the Jefferson County fairgrounds.

I arrived on Tuesday evening of the second week of the County Fair in Jefferson Grove, population 42,592— the largest city in the county. This was the highlight of the year for so many people from all parts of the county. It was the time for those from outlying agricultural regions to display the fruits of their hard work in the excellent new barns the city had built. This meant trucking into town all kinds of livestock—cows, hogs, goats, sheep, and all kinds of fancy-feathered birds—along with the supplies needed to maintain the animals and the farmers themselves for up to two weeks as they vied for blue ribbons, bartered with competitors, and swapped genetic information. For the young folks there was the opportunity to meet new people from outside their small farm communities. And if they were lucky and adventurous, there were secret places to meet after the giant machines rested and the colored lights surrendered the night to the moon and the stars.

As host to the annual event, the city of Jefferson Grove anticipated a considerable profit. The hotels and restaurants saw this as the occasion to make up for slow spring and winter seasons, and vendors of the traditional fare— candy apples, waffles, sausage, pizza, cotton candy, and beer—would always do well. Residents near the fairgrounds took in wads of money from the people who wanted close parking spots, and there was plenty of overtime work available for the police and emergency crews.

For both the city and the farm people there would be opportunities to display their particular talents by competing in various events, including demolition derbies, dirt-bike jumping contests, art displays, and cheerleading competitions. Carnies in the gaming tents would shout their bold and often rude challenges to the fairgoers to try their luck at dart throwing, duck picking, water pistol shooting, basketball shooting, and baseball throwing.

As for the carnival workers—those transients who traveled town to town with the fair—the residents of Jefferson County held various opinions. There were the snobbish sorts, the ones who regarded carnies as a tribe of incestuous vagabonds, unclean misfits, and ne'er-do-wells. Some residents were afraid of them, and would double lock their doors during the fair weeks. But there was another group, characterized by the more adventurous and young-at-heart, who saw the "carnies" as free spirits, not bound to anyone or any place. They were the modern-day, flesh-and-blood representatives of the Gypsies and Bohemians of films and novels. And they were the assemblers of the colorful tents and the phantasmagoric machinery that lit the nights for two straight weeks every year.

One of the most anticipated and highly attended events at the fair was the Battle of the Bands, which was always scheduled on the Friday night during the first week of the fair. Several bands from across the county competed, and for the past ten years, Bernard Bauer had been one of the judges.

III

Mayor Bill Swank took his place behind his very large desk and introduced me to Paul Hadley, Chief of Police, and Melissa Reardon, owner of a dance studio and a city board member. Miss Reardon also was a judge at the Battle of the Bands the previous Friday night. She was greatly concerned about the assault on Bernard Bauer, whom she described as an important representative of the Jefferson Grove business community.

"Listen, Mr. James," said the mayor assertively, his eyebrows leaping half way up his forehead (a tic, I supposed). "We appreciate your agency's cooperation in sending you here on such short notice. We were informed that you have a keen eye and will likely get to the bottom of what happened last Friday night. Mr. Bauer is well-respected in our city. To be frank, it is hard to imagine any reason for his abduction other than that someone didn't want him to judge at the Battle of the Bands." He punctuated this display of logic with two leaps of the eyebrows.

"That's right," said Miss Reardon, her small but fit figure swelling with an air of indignance. "Bernard has participated in the show for ten years now, and he has the musical knowledge and the experience to be an excellent judge of talent. Obviously, if someone didn't want him judging, then that person likely has very little talent. I would look at the thrash metal band first. They are a bunch of loud, unruly thugs who like to make trouble."

"Hold your horses now, Melissa," interjected Officer Hadley. "I'm sure Mr. James will inspect matters according to his agency's protocol. "Let's let him do his job. For us, let's focus on this coming Friday's rematch and make sure it all goes off without a hitch."

Miss Reardon replied coldly, her nose wrinkling as if she had smelled something unpleasant. "The worst incident would be someone less than our best representing Jefferson Grove at the state competition next month."

The mayor leaned forward, placing his hands on his big desk and looking straight at me as he began to explain what had happened last Friday. "There are usually five judges at the show, Mr. James. Since Bernard was not there, that left only four, an even number. It turned out that each judge picked a different winner, and not one would budge in favor of another band. So the contest ended in a draw. Now that's a problem!" he exclaimed. "You see, the winner not only gets the $2000.00 award, but also an invitation to go to the state competition in Columbus." He clenched two fists on the tabletop, his eyebrows now triple-leaping with suspense. "That, Mr. James, is a big deal! There are talent agents from New York and Nashville, all looking for the next Taylor Swift. We just might have her right here in Jefferson Grove." (I wondered if it was a foregone conclusion that a female would represent Jefferson county.)

The decision had already been made to replay the battle on Friday, two nights before the closing of the fair. Chief Hadley and his department would see to it personally that all five judges made it safely to the event. Meanwhile, I had a lot of ground to cover over the next two days.

IV

It appeared that Bernard Bauer lived a pretty normal life. He was middle-aged, married, and had one kid in middle school. He quit teaching music at the elementary school after just a few years, apparently having no love for the profession. He then bought the music store with an investment from his well-to-do parents. For a short while he played guitar in a quartet, but never really took to it. The turning point in his career was when the only other music store in town burned down. He seized the opportunity to expand his business and Bauer Music began to prosper.

He was still at home recovering from the assault when I arrived at the store, leaving two young sales reps in charge. It was a traditional music store. One wall was hung with colorful guitars of various makes and models. An array of brand-new amplifiers lined the floor underneath them. A separate room featured three sets of drums and a glass cabinet full of sundry rhythm instruments and electronic gadgets. There was another section that held racks of sheet music, above which hung shiny brass instruments. An additional room in the back contained keyboards (there were no real pianos) along with stacks of PA equipment and stage lighting.

One of the clerks explained that their customer base consisted of several different types. Much of the business came from the public schools—parents scraped up the money to buy or rent instruments for their kids to participate in school ensembles. For some parents and their kids it was an exciting prospect. For others it was an unpleasant obligation, and a money pit of repair costs and nagging upgrades.

Then there were the aspiring rock players—guitarists, bassists, and drummers who were eager to try out their rudimentary skills in the store and had to be monitored closely by the employees lest they get carried away with their "jamming" and disturb the paying customers.

Not all the rockers were so underdeveloped, however. According to the store clerk, there was a strong core of those interested in classic rock, especially the 80's variety. This was the music their grandparents listened to on the radio, and many young kids with busy or absent parents were exposed to a lot of 80's pop rock growing up through their grandparents. The music crossed generations, creating a bond based on what the old folk insisted was the greatest American music. For so many of these affluent or middle-class white kids, it also meant the opportunity to periodically upgrade by purchasing more expensive equipment, much to the benefit of Bernard Bauer.

Another group of frequent visitors to Bauer Music consisted of older, more established players in the area—keyboardists, horn players, drummers, and bass players who had played semi-professionally over the years. This was a frugal bunch, preferring to look for deals on the internet rather than buy from the store. They came there to chat about equipment, to tout new releases of their favorite artists, and to drop names of semi-famous artists they had been remotely connected to in the past. This was sometimes annoying to the employees, and especially to Bernard, who wished they would shut up and buy something.

Then there were the softer voices of some of those young musicians, many of them acoustic guitar-strumming neo-hippie types who dreamed up original songs that spoke to their loneliness, their feeling of injustice, or their need to be heard and understood in this harsh and judgmental world. Sometimes they would vent, shouting epithets about ex-mates and hitting the strings hard to show their resolve. They typically bought strings, picks, and maybe a capo. If Bernard was lucky, one would leave with a new guitar. "A beautiful voice like yours," he would say, "deserves a guitar to match."

It was apparent that Mr. Bauer made a pretty good living through his store, and, in one way or another, he was familiar with most of the groups that he would judge during the Battle of the Bands rematch this coming Friday night. With regard to my investigation, it became clear that I would need to interview each of the four competing bands, and I would need to do it soon.

V

The heavy metal/thrash rock band *Euranus* rehearsed in a huge, dilapidated dairy barn in a rural community twelve miles east of Jefferson Grove, just a few miles past the junkyard where Bauer was found tied to the Ferris wheel cradle. There was a loud rumbling sound coming from the barn as I pulled up the driveway. Realizing that no one would be able to hear my knocking, I searched for an entrance. At length I found a hole in the wall where the old clapboards had been punched out. As I entered, I felt something at my ankles—a strange, rubbery, nibbling sensation. I turned and looked down to see a pointy-eared pink pig with a dirty snout snuffling around my feet! There was a sudden silence of the drumming. "Peter!" hollered one of the players, "be nice to the man."

"That's Peter the Pig," said a heavy set, powerful-looking red-haired boy in a yellow "wife-beater" tank top. Zach, the leader of the band, rose from his drum seat there on the barn floor beneath the hayloft. "And who are you?"

I introduced myself and explained what my purpose was, which seemed to amuse Zach. He motioned for me to join them.

The interior of the barn was lit by slanted beams of sunlight piercing through the walls like so many fingers. Motes of dust swirled within the rays that illuminated a series of large speakers lined up along the milking stalls. In the middle of it all Zach sat like a king on his throne amid his neon red drum set, replete with two kick drums, two floor toms, two mounted toms, two cowbells, four cymbals, and a jumbo snare.

"Pete's a greedy little bastard, and he's mad lately because he knows all them beauty pageant pigs is in town for the fair, and we don't let him go."

Zach then introduced me to the other two players. Twin brothers Roger Wills, the bass player, and Duke Wills, the guitarist, were tall and lanky, about 6'8" and less than 200 pounds each. Their hair was wavy and dyed gold, cascading over their shoulders and accenting the metallic hoop piercings of their nose and lips. The fourth band member, lead singer Timothy, had not shown up for practice, and the boys claimed that they had no idea where he was.

I asked them if they knew anything about Mr. Bauer and the Friday night incident.

Roger, feigning serious concern, offered his analysis first: "Yeah, man, I heard about that. Poor dude got bagged and snatched. What a bad trip, man."

More insight came from his twin Duke: "Yeah, a free trip to the countryside. The dude got dumped at the dump! But I guess he got recycled!" The brothers laughed in unison.

Thankfully, Zach took over. "Seriously, man, all we can tell you is that Bernie Bauer is a slick and sleazy dude—when he shakes your hand with one hand, he's got the other in your pocket." While he spoke, the twins were giggling and whispering the words to "Aqualung," the 1971 FM hit by Jethro Tull.

"We don't deal with Bauer. Anyway, we already knew he wouldn't vote for us, and we never expected to win, what with no true metalheads on the judge panel. We just wanted to stir things up, you know, have some fun at the fair. In fact, we were surprised to get the one vote. So you see, there was no incentive for us to hurt the man"

As I left the barn, Peter the pig followed, sniffing at my feet, and then rising on his tiptoes to higher regions, which caused me to turn and walk backwards. "Get back here, Peter, you little shit head" hollered Zach as I reached the safety of my car.

Later that evening I drove to a posh community of three-story Tudor and Victorian homes with long driveways in the up-river section of Jefferson Grove. *Gold 'n Moments*, the classic rock band fronted by Lisa Goldman, was rehearsing in the studio upstairs of the garage of one of those fine homes. Her father, Harold Goldman, interrupted the practice to introduce me as an investigator into the very serious crime that had been committed.

Lisa certainly had the look of a rock star, with purple and black spiky hair and a swaggering stance. And, at 17 or 18 years old and wearing a short skirt and a tight-fitting tank top advertising her more-than-ample breasts, she glowed in comparison to her band mates who, despite their long hair and spandex pants, did not appear young. Lisa readily agreed with her father that the kidnapping was a brutal and vengeful act, but that neither she nor her group members had any clue as to who might have done it.

On Thursday I drove down river to one of the project homes where *Lay Zee and the Bones* were supposed to be practicing. Rapper Larry Z-Jones was in a complaining mood, as only one of the four Bones (his all-female supporting cast of singers and dancers-with-an-attitude) had arrived. He said to her, "Maria, Mr. James here got some questions about old Bernie the Banker. Was it you who tripped him? And, say, where them ho's at anyway? The show is tomorrow, don't they know that?"

"I don't know where they is," said Maria. "Maybe they found some real man who got real money. Put some meat on they bones. As far as that kidnapping goes, I got a solid alibi, all us girls do. We was all at the beauty shop getting our hair done for the show. And that's a fact." She winked at me. "But I don't know about Larry Z, here, she said smiling. He got a mean steak in him."

Larry smiled, then laughed outright. "See what I have to deal with, Mr. James. I get no respect. But anyway, I have no idea what happened to the man. Sorry I can't help you. And by the way, hope you make it to the show tomorrow. We gonna make yo jaw drop, dog!"

My last stop was in the riverfront zone, a middle to lower middle-class neighborhood of one-story ranch style homes not far from the fairgrounds. Large weeping willows and oaks dominated the area, casting the streets and the riverfront in a dark green hue at twilight. In the driveway of the house was a shiny-clean classic car—an olive-green '69 Chrysler Imperial, one of the widest rides ever manufactured in the States. As I parked in the street, I could hear the band *Premonition* rehearsing somewhere in the house.

Mrs. Karina Jones answered the front door. Her daughter, Jessica, was the lead singer and guitarist for the band.

"That's quite a car you have there," I said after introducing myself.

"Why thank you. It was my husband's. It's been sitting, and I suppose I ought to do something with it," she mused. "Anyhow, the band just got started, but I'm sure they won't mind an audience."

Mrs. Jones led me down into the basement where I listened to them run through the three songs they would do at the competition. They worked meticulously on dynamics, arrangements, and endings. Two songs were originals, the third a hypnotic rendering of Sting's "All This Time". The band had an eclectic and original sound, infused with elements of old-school rhythm & blues, ska, and jazz.

After the run-through, I asked Jessica about Bernard Bauer. She looked away nervously, deferring to her keyboard player, Josh. "None of us go there much," he said. "His prices are high, and it's kinda, well, not exactly the kind of vibe we can relate to. But we had nothing against him. Certainly no reason to wrap him up."

On my way out, Mrs. Jones invited me for a drink. It seemed like she might have something to disclose, so I followed her behind the house, down to where the trees lined the edge of the river. There between the gazebo and the water, lit up by a flood light, was an amazing sculpture—a five-foot tall scale model of a Ferris wheel, replete with sixteen spokes and tubs, support posts, and exit stairs.

We sat in the gazebo, at first small-talking about the band and the upcoming battle while drinking some homemade wine, which was surprisingly good. She had a lovely and enchanting speaking voice—one that ranged from light to dark in tone, always rhythmic in her phrasing. I guessed that her daughter inherited that quality and applied it to her singing. At length we got on to the topic of Bernard Bauer.

VI

"My husband John, bless his soul, was a mechanic, and also a part-time musician, a fine trumpet and piano player. He worked for a while with Bauer, who played guitar. John never cared for him, I have to say. Said he wasn't much of a player, and then he wasn't much of a teacher either, so he became a businessman, booking his own band and then opening the store. John said it seemed like there was always funny money with the gigs they played. One time when the weather was real bad and John showed up ten minutes late—he'd slid off the road—Bauer docked half his pay at the end of the night. Strange thing was, after John died in that car wreck, Bernard started coming around here, saying he would be glad to help out Jessica any way he could, and even offered free lessons.

"Well, Jessica advanced beyond him real fast, but then she just quit lessons all of a sudden, and stopped practicing. She never did say why, but I suppose it didn't matter because, after a few months she picked up the guitar again and went at it on her own with a vengeance. She practiced for hours every day after school, learning songs by ear from recordings."

While Mrs. Jones was speaking, I noticed a strange sound coming from the riverbank, something like a small motorboat in the distance. Now it had become more prominent, and seemingly much closer—a humming sound. Mrs. Jones paused in recognition.

"Hello there Herbie," she called into the trees. "This is Mr. James. Why don't you come and join us?" Then slowly, very cautiously, a small man stepped out from the shadows onto the lawn. He couldn't have been more than four feet tall.

With nervous hesitation the little man came and sat on the stool by Mrs. Jones, his legs dangling there, his tight, boy-size shirt revealing a very muscular frame. It was soon apparent that Herbie did not talk. Instead, he made humming sounds that accelerated and decelerated with the rate of his breathing. After a while he settled into a soft purring.

"Mr. James," she said, "it seems you are a decent man, or else Herbie would not have come out. So, will you let me tell you his story?

"There was a time when the fair was more like a real carnival, before it turned into the kind of commercial, family friendly, politically correct display of techno-entertainment that it is today. Back then it was more like a traveling show featuring some of the most unique and rare people on the planet. A freak show, some called it. There was the Human Blockhead, who pounded nails into his head and up his nose, there was the Bearded Lady, there was Swamp Boy who was raised by snakes, and the Sword Swallower, and the Monkey Girl... What a strange little pocket of humanity! But I believe those were the ones who gave us lasting memories, and something to talk about even to this day. Nowadays, I don't think kids remember much about the fair. For so many of them, it's more like a life-size video game."

She paused, looking fondly at Herbie who rocked gently on his stool as if entranced by her voice. "My apologies for the heavy dose of nostalgia. So, I was talking about Herbie, who you probably have guessed by now does not speak. But he has his strengths. In fact, he was billed as 'The World's Strongest Boy'. And there was truth in that. At ten years old he could lift more than almost any man. On top of that, he stopped growing in height—nobody knows why, he just got stuck at the height he is now, which enabled the show to go on for several years. Part of the act involved challenges by the men in the audience, who bet money for the chance to beat him. But Herbie could bench press over 400 pounds. He could out-squat, out-curl, out-shotput just about any man. For a few years, it all went well for Herbie, and for his manager and guardian, an eccentric entertainer who called himself Scarecrow.

"Scarecrow was the emcee for the traveling show. He possessed a powerful announcer's voice that could cut through the noise of the fair. Old Scarecrow was also a drunk, sometimes a mean drunk, and sometimes he would go missing for a few days to get straight. Then he'd be on the wagon for a while, but that never lasted long.

"Down deep, Scarecrow had a good heart, and he always looked out for the performers, especially the misfits. He adopted Herbie and Cora—the Monkey Girl. Cora, God rest her soul. She was blind, but she could climb anything. You should have seen her in her glory days—the featured act in the Big Top where she performed on a huge and elaborate set of monkey bars. What an incredible display of grace and agility!

"Everything was great for a while, but it was only a matter of time before Herbie's act went downhill. After a while people had seen it too many times, and especially when Herbie got older and grew facial hair and looked more like a little man than a boy, the novelty wore off.

"It was here in Jefferson Grove that old Scarecrow drank himself to death the night after Cora fell to her death from the high bars. Herbie, who was just fourteen years old, had now lost a sister and father figure inside a week. He had nobody to watch out for him.

"My husband was an excellent mechanic, and he could fix more than just cars. His garage was close to the fairgrounds, and during the fair he was on-call to repair everything from trucks to trailers to the amusement rides. That's how he got to know Herbie. Herbie and John grew really close working on those machines. When it became clear that Herbie's strongman performances at the fair were becoming passé, John decided to hire him year-round at the garage. Basically, we adopted Herbie.

Herbie really took to the work at the garage. He was so strong, he could lift motors, and being so small he could get into places others couldn't. On weekend nights, he'd go with John to his music gigs, carrying all the heavy equipment. When Jessica was born, Herbie took on the big brother role. He was always so protective of her. And Jessica loved him just as much. We were a fine family.

"But then when John died, Herbie seemed to take it harder than any of us. I didn't know what to do with him anymore. He was so restless, so empty-hearted, and he couldn't seem to focus on any job he found. Without John, he was lost here in this town. He couldn't speak it, but I saw in his eyes that he needed to move on, to get back to the life he knew as a child—life in the carnival."

It was dark now in the gazebo, and the little Ferris Wheel glinted in the starlight, turning slowly in the gentle breeze. I could see Mrs. Jones was crying. Herbie sat faithfully by her side, now holding her hand.

"Well, I've kept you too long, Mr. James," she said, straightening herself. "And Herbert, you need to get back to the fairgrounds." Turning to me she explained, "Herbert works on the rides there, does the assembly and maintenance on the Ferris wheel and other rides. People say the Big Wheel wouldn't be safe without him."

As I was leaving, I asked about the Ferris wheel sculpture on the lawn.

"Cora and Herbert made that from scrap metal—parts of bikes and farm equipment and metal scraps that Herbie found for her. You see, part of her act—the finale, you could say—was to climb the Ferris wheel on the last day of the fair. Even though she was blind, her sense of touch was so keen that she could recreate objects through her tactile memory. Amazing, isn't it?"

VII

Because *The Tower* assigned me this case at the last minute during the fair, there were no available rooms nearby. Mayor Swank had managed to get me into a sleazy motel in the projects area called the Buffalo Nickel Inn. The room smelled of chlorine and urine and stale cigarette smoke, and the curtains and the bedspread, made of the same floral designed material, were heavy and stiff. Outside my window, glistening in the steady rain, the large Buffalo-head sign loomed in the night, its plastic panels partially broken by the wind, the colors faded. Yet there was enough light to see across the parking lot to the last room at the far end of the strip.

I was restless that night. The sad stories of the carnival, of Herbie and his families, stirred up memories of my own. The threat of recurring nightmares kept me up past midnight. The rain had stopped, leaving a soft mist in the air as I looked out my window into the half-lit parking lot. It was then I saw a small Honda pull into the lot and proceed to the far end. A man and a woman, both in hoodies, darted from the car and into the last room. Then came a second car—a sprawling, low-riding antique I recognized as the Imperial in Mrs. Jones' yard earlier that day. It cruised slowly to the end of the motel like a cat stalking its prey, then pulled off into a muddy field behind the buildings and parked there, out of sight.

About twenty minutes later, the couple in hoodies returned to their car, this time not so discreetly. The female was waving her arms, apparently angry about something, while the male tried to calm her down. Suddenly, they both turned toward the field where the Imperial was parked as if they had heard or seen something there. Then there was a flash of light, and another. I could read the lips of the female as she turned toward the man: "What the fuck was that?"

As the Honda raced out of the parking lot and down the streets of the projects, the olive-green Imperial rolled lazily from the field, its massive front grill grinning like a Cheshire cat. I ran downstairs and opened the door to see who was driving. But for one small hand on the wheel, it seemed no one was driving at all.

VIII

Early the next morning, I returned to the home of Karina Jones. Jessica was already up and going over the lyrics to her songs. Karina looked as if she half-expected me as I stood there by the Imperial, which was muddy and had been moved to a different spot.

"Well, Mr. James, I guess someone must have stolen it last night, or I should say took it for a joy ride. You know how easy it is to hotwire these old cars."

I pointed out to her that the keys were in the ignition, to which she responded, "Oh my goodness. I must have left them there by accident! Please, Mr. James, feel free to inspect the car for any kind of evidence. Let me just say that I'm glad it was returned, and I need to get ready for work, if you don't mind."

She winked and left me to my business.

IX

Among all the lit-up machinery across the fairway, the Ferris Wheel stood tallest and brightest. The colorful, shiny pods that held riders had faded into the twilight, and now the spokes of the great wheel glowed neon green, white, blue and red. I thought of Herbie there, beneath the slow and powerful cycling, in the heart of the great machine, making sure gears were greased, its motor running smoothly.

It was Friday night, and the grandstands were starting to fill up for the Battle of the Bands, Part II. Mayor Swank invited me to sit with him in the judge's booth. As he introduced me to the judges, the leaps of his eyebrows communicated that he was proud of the diversity represented here. City board member and dance teacher Melissa Reardon sat on the end, tapping her pencil impatiently. Next to her was an Hispanic male, a councilman from the projects. The third judge was a male storekeeper from an outlying farming community. Fourth was a female African American history teacher from the high school. Last was Bernard Bauer, who looked rather nervous, and was not very talkative. I took a seat behind him.

First up in the Battle of the Bands was *Lay Zee and the Bones*. As the lights came on, the Bones girls stood motionless, one at each of the four corners of the stage. They were wrapped in robes, like the one worn by the Statue of Liberty, and were holding candles in the air. In the middle of the stage was Lay Zee, who lay inside a box—a coffin—during the initial silence. The audience hushed in anticipation.

Then, as the soundtrack beats grew louder, the girls began to move, very suggestively, soon doffing their wraps to reveal curvaceous bodies clad in very shiny and colorful underwear. They surrounded the coffin, shaking and gyrating as they bowed up and down, waving life into it. Slowly and mechanically, Lay Zee rose out of the box, microphone in hand. He began to strut and fret around the stage, as if confused. After a couple minutes of this drama, he gathered up his swagger, faced the audience, and began his rap, the words of which were difficult to understand in the echoing stadium. As the music intensified, so did his rapping and the girls' dancing around him. It reached its climax as he raised both arms and waved away the girls. He had apparently tired of them, causing them to retreat reluctantly to the four corners of the stage. In the waning minutes, Lay Zee mellowed down, then returned to his bed, apparently happy to be rid of the girls. As the beats slowed and faded, the Bones girls came from their corners and surrounded the sleeping Lay Zee. They appeared to weep as they covered the coffin with their wraps.

The audience was thrilled by the performance, which lasted about ten minutes. In the judge's booth, only the man from the projects seemed impressed. Certainly, Melissa Reardon was not. She shook her head and scratched at her judge's card.

Next up was *Euranus* to perform their 12-minute original song called "Analhilation," which promised to be a stark contrast to the previous act. Barechested Zach sat like a sultan at his enormous drum set. Roger and Duke stood like twin towers on either side of him, their wild hair cascading over the strings of their guitars. Timothy, who was absent when I visited the barn, turned out to be a short and vibrant young black man.

It is hard to describe their performance. It was sheer power, but not without some grace and complexity. The boys played fast and furious behind Timothy, who somehow managed to sing over the top of the band. His voice soared like a powerful bird amid the storm of their music. In conclusion, they crushed it, literally, as the twins toppled their amplifiers and began stomping on them while continuing to play, which created some wild, screeching feedback. Zach, unleashing his extra-large sticks, punched holes into his drum skins and smashed two of his cymbals into pieces! All the while Timothy ran around the stage, prodding them on like a mad anarchist.

If all that wasn't enough, there was the sudden appearance from backstage of Peter the Pig, who tip-toed forward dressed in "wife-beater" shirt. Despite the pandemonium, Peter went about the business of sniffing out some French fries that had been thrown onto the stage.

As *Euranus* took their bows, some of the crowd went wild, shouting for an encore (which was not feasible since their equipment had been destroyed). Meanwhile, the judges stared wide-eyed, dumbfounded by the phenomenon they had just witnessed. There was a half hour delay in the show while a work crew cleaned up the fallout from *Euranus*. Then *Premonition* took the stage. As I had witnessed at their rehearsal, the band was tight, and the players were individually talented and expressive. They performed their three songs flawlessly. Jessica Johnson was stellar, playing leads that were at once majestically melodic and rhythmically complex. Yet it was her voice that struck me as the most unique and wonderful aspect of the entire show.

The audience reacted positively, but with diminished enthusiasm (*Euranus* was a tough act to follow). The judges, having mostly recovered from "Anal-hi-lation," marked their cards prudently. At last it was time for *Gold 'n Moments*, the classic rock band led by local rock diva Lisa Goldman. She was stunning in her Madonna-inspired fishnet hosiery, sequined bra-top and spike heels. The first song was a strict cover of Heart's "Barracuda," which the band performed well. Lisa Goldman sounded very much like Ann Wilson as she strutted back and forth across the stage. They followed up with an original written by Lisa herself entitled "Love is all I Feel," an anthem ballad about longing for someone who had moved away to Hollywood for fame and glory. Last was a version of Billy Ocean's "Get Out of my Dreams and Into My Car," in which Lisa pranced about the stage as she sang, sometimes pretending to be turning a steering wheel.

There was a strong reaction from the crowd as *Gold n' Moments* finished their set. As was customary for the event, the judges would take a short pause, then reconvene to deliberate and choose a winner.

During the break, I asked Bernard Bauer if I could speak with him for a moment in private. Walking with him toward the men's room, I pulled from my pocket the photograph I had found in the front seat while searching the '69 Imperial that morning. I handed it to him. "This must be yours," I said. "You can keep it—don't worry, I have a copy." Mr. Bauer turned ghostly white as he saw himself and Lisa Goldman outside the motel, their faces clearly exposed by the camera despite their hoodies.

I continued. "We'll keep this between us, Mr. Bauer, but I have two favors to ask of you. First, drop all the investigation into your kidnapping. Tell them you must have been drunk, or someone slipped you a drug. You figure it out. Second, regarding this competition, you have only two choices. Cast your ballot for either *Euranus* or *Lay Zee*."

A few minutes later the judging panel cast their votes.

"Ladies and Gentlemen," announced Mayor Bill Swank into the microphone, his voice wavering as it echoed back from the grandstand, his eyebrows leaping like lunatic lizards, "the winner of this year's Jefferson County Battle of the Bands is (he paused, glancing at Melissa Reardon whose face looked like she could kill someone) is *Euranus*."

The audience response was a roaring, hellish mixture of cheers and boos. Police Chief Paul Hadley mobilized his force to intervene in case the scene turned violent.

X
———

Before I left Jefferson Grove, I paid a visit to Mrs. Jones, who was in the front yard with Jessica and Chief Hadley inspecting the Chrysler Imperial. "Paul is thinking about buying the old beast," she said brightly.

"But what I want to know, Karina," said the officer, "is whether this camera here comes with it."

"I'll have to think about that," she replied coyly.

Upon my leaving, I assured them that, as far as I was concerned, this case was closed. I also told them that I had a powerful dream last night, a kind of 'premonition': Jessica Jones was destined to become a great musician, a star who would perform major shows all over the world. Also in the dream was a quiet and powerful little man who worked as her lead roadie.

The Invisible Knife

I

"I want to know once and for all who did this to me!" hollered Hugh Jackson III, waving his stubbed hands dramatically for all to witness (and seeming to startle himself more than the rest of us). This was the climax of a speech he had prepared for me and the local policemen on the morning of my arrival in New Iberia, LA. I had come to investigate a six-month old case that remained unsolved, largely because there were no credible witnesses, or at least none willing to come forward with any kind of evidence regarding the gruesome dismemberment of all ten of Mr. Jackson's fingers last October. The incident was shrouded in a heap of contradictory testimony which included several accounts of inexplicable and/or supernatural events. There was yet to be found any real evidence.

It was a beautiful April morning in southern Louisiana. After the meeting, Police Chief Bobby Doucet offered to give me a tour of the region. He seemed to think it was important for me to get a sense of the lay of the land and the local culture. Doucet was over six feet tall. He had black, wavy hair that seemed too long for a cop. Despite the constraints of his uniform, it was apparent that Doucet was in excellent physical shape—a forty-year-old man in a twenty-year-old's body. His dark Cajun eyes, indigenous to these wetlands, were in perpetual motion as we drove south toward the Gulf.

We traveled twenty-five miles to Lake Martin Reserve, where it was mating season for various species of herons and ibis and other wading birds. I had never seen anything as strangely magnificent as those bald cypresses rising out of the swamps, hung now with the plump and pointed forms of thousands of pink, white, red, blue, and black birds. We walked along the path that bordered the lake, our voices rising over the cacophony of the birds' spring ritual. Eventually, we entered a darker, quieter area, where the trees were larger, the foliage denser, and the birds much fewer. We came upon a small clearing along the swamp's edge in the middle of which was a very large tree. On its sharp and crooked branches, three great birds sat facing each other—one scarlet, one black, and one white—forming a kind of triangle. Spanish moss hung like drapery from branches surrounding them, as if enclosing them in a secret room. It seemed to me these strange birds resided within a silence separate from the world around them.

II

I learned from Bobby Doucet that Judge Hugh Jackson III came from a wealthy family, a line of sugar cane farmers who, over the course of five generations, had expanded their acreage to cover nearly a third of the Parish. The family also had a reputation for exerting influence throughout the region, producing numerous public and political figures, including judges, lawyers, insurance company executives, and state representatives. Hugh was the grandson and namesake of one very influential judge, Hugh Jackson I, who presided over some of the highest profile cases of KKK and other race-related crimes during the 1930's. A self-declared independent, Hugh Jackson I was not beholden to any political entity. His highest moral principal was founded solely in his ambition to expand the interests of family enterprise. Thus, he became a powerful man in Iberia Parish.

Hugh Jackson III was a man of similar ambition. Though he never married or had children, he grew the family business by using government grants to purchase 500 acres of farmland a few miles north of town. He contracted with a major fracking company from Oklahoma. Within the first year there were already a half dozen drill rigs in place, some towering 150 feet above the cleared land. Although no gas had yet been discovered, the judge was confident they would hit the jackpot eventually, which he claimed would be a great boon to the local economy. High tide lifts all boats, he was fond of saying.

Meanwhile, farmers in the area were having troubles with their wells, and there were numerous reports of underground rumblings, some that would shake the shingles off the houses. Their complaints, of course, fell on deaf ears.

The judge lived alone with his guard-dog rottweiler in a manor west of the town. Separated from the public roads by a white fence, his seventy acres were meticulously tended to by a small landscaping company. The expansive lawn was kept smooth and green. Live oaks and myrtle crepes lined the series of driveways connecting the house and the barns. Small shanties—the living quarters of slaves and sharecroppers during a bygone era—were set back away from the drive. They stood empty now, but were well preserved in the proud tradition of the antebellum South.

There was, however, one particular eyesore, something that chronically disturbed the judge. On the east end of the property, about two hundred yards from the mansion itself, a twenty-acre patch of undisturbed wilderness separated the Judge's great lawn from a public road. Within those dense, vine-tangled woods was a half-acre clearing. In the middle of the clearing sat a single cottage occupied by a peculiar woman with wild black hair. Her name was Emma Montaigne.

Rumors swirled regarding the nature of this woman and her relations with the Judge. What became most clear and relevant, however, was that her family once owned much of the property that is now the Judge's. Furthermore, the cottage was once adjunct to a third house and its forty acres. The main house caught fire twenty years ago, when Emma was five years old. While her mother, two sisters, and Emma watched the conflagration helplessly from the distance, her father tried to enter the house to retrieve a sum of cash money hidden inside. The walls collapsed around him, and the cash burned along with the father. It was later determined that the fire was caused by one of the girls playing with matches.

The nearest neighbor and owner of the mansion, Judge Jackson III, offered his deeply felt condolences, along with a seemingly fair price to buy all the property. Much to the judge's chagrin, the girls' mother agreed to sell only half the land and insisted on keeping the twenty acres surrounding the cottage on the east end, where she resided.

Having lost all their savings in the fire and working now as a waitress in town, the mother ran into problems caring for three young girls. She sent one daughter, Estela, to live with an uncle in Jeanette, about ten miles away. The second daughter, Veronica, who was assumed to have started the fire, was sent to a cousin's family in New Orleans. The third sister, Emma, would stay with her mother in the cottage, which she and her sisters would inherit upon her mother's passing ten years later.

"So you see," said Chief Doucet, "life in the South is not as simple as you might think."

It was clear that I would need to pay a visit to Emma Montaigne and her little plot of wilderness.

III

As I got out of Doucet's air conditioned patrol car at my motel in downtown New Iberia, I couldn't help but swoon; it felt like I walked into an over-heated sauna. The chief smiled at my reaction, then suggested we take a ride later that evening when it would be cooler. He suggested the Whiskey River Landing, an authentic Cajun bar and restaurant on the Atchafalaya River. I agreed, thankful for the opportunity to rest and let the heat of the late afternoon pass.

He picked me up that evening not in his patrol car, but in a 1969 yellow Thunderbird— very impressive. We drove twenty miles north along the river and its bayous. The landing sat right on the waterfront, surrounded by fishing boats that rocked gently on the muddy waters. The bar was lit up brightly, pulsating with the compelling beat of a zydeco band. We entered into the pungent aroma of down-home Louisiana cooking—crawfish and crabs and shrimp and all those spices that go into gumbo and jambalaya. Half the people were eating and drinking in booths along the perimeter of the large, hard-wood dance floor. The other half were out on the floor performing variations of the two-step.

As I watched the dancers, I was impressed with how they were able to move so effortlessly all over the wood floor, their heads never bobbing up or down, always parallel to the floor, eyes locked in a kind of stoic embrace. Despite the variety of color of skin and texture of hair among these people, there seemed to be a kind of homogeny, a blending together, as if they were all of the same clan. Here was a rare place in America that had resisted popular culture and somehow managed to retain a unique identity. Its history seemed to be alive in the present moment.

Bobby was a bachelor. He was from these parts and everyone seemed to know him. Moreover, despite his law enforcement position, he liked to drink, and there were many women who were happy to drink with him. I watched as he two-stepped with several different partners, all of whom seemed reluctant to let him go. His prominent Adam's apple undulated as he danced effortlessly with eyes half-closed—he was a lean and sculpted figure, a boyish man, and a rare combination of strength and grace.

I learned that Bobby was once a defensive back at LSU, made all conference, and was drafted by the New Orleans Saints in the third round. As a pro, he soon discovered he didn't have the kind of heart (or mindset) to propel his body recklessly head-on into the path of a 250-pound running back who had gained a full head of steam. After two seasons as a back-up safety and special teams player, Bobby had had enough. He returned home to his roots and quickly advanced through the ranks of the local police.

We drank and ate well that night. I was especially struck by our waitress, who, surprisingly paid more attention to me than to Bobby. Bobby introduced her to me as Jean Blanchet. She was probably in her early thirties, and beyond her charming southern belle accent and cat-like black eyes, she wore her cut-off shorts extremely well. I made up my mind that I would return here to the Whiskey River Landing.

It was after midnight when Bobby dropped me off at my motel room at the end of Main Street. The night was relatively cool and offered a fair breeze, so I decided to take a walk through town. The storefronts were dark, the dimly lit streets empty. A half-moon shrouded in grey clouds illuminated the sidewalk. Suddenly I heard what sounded like a shuffling of feet as I passed an alleyway. I glimpsed a fleeting silhouette of something as large as a human, but it seemed to move on four legs. It must have been the booze, I told myself. Moreover, it had been a long day and I was in strange territory. I picked up my pace and returned to my room. Just as I was closing my door, I heard it again—a strange shuffling in the little patch of woods behind the motel.

IV

The next day, I met Bobby at a little café downtown, where he filled me in on what was known along with what was not known regarding the mysterious dismemberment of Judge Jackson's fingers.

It happened during the wee hours of a moonlit night after the Judge had been awakened by what he described as an "eerie wailing" in his back yard. Accompanied by his Rottweiler—which apparently never barked at the sound—he ventured outside. All he remembers is that he tripped over something, then woke up some time later in severe pain. He must have passed out again in shock as he saw what had happened to his hands. He was discovered about 7:00 a.m. by his nephew, who had called the ambulance. Doctors at the hospital were incredulous. They were unable to explain why there was so little blood, and how there was relatively little infection considering the severity of the cutting. The only thing the police could figure out was that whatever the weapon was, it was extremely sharp, and whoever wielded it demonstrated incredible skill. But perhaps the strangest thing of all was that his dog just disappeared. No one has a clue what happened to it.

Bobby informed me he needed to tend to his regular duties and would not accompany me to Emma Montaigne's cottage. He sighed as he sat back in his chair. "This woman is unusual," he understated. "I have had little contact with her, and she rarely talks to anyone. The town people, especially the ones who live on the outskirts, are protective of her because they believe she is a healer of some sort. Rumor has it she has done miracles with animals, cured them of injuries and disease that should have killed them. That sort of thing. So, I don't know what you are going to learn when you meet her, but I can tell you another real sad story about Emma and her family.

"His name's John Lagarde—pure creole, real dark and strong as an ox. And he's a man of few words. But I don't believe there are any words that could express his love for Emma. He first met her when she was just a little girl, nine years old, four years after the fire near the plantation. John was 17 then, and he worked for Judge Jackson as a landscaper. One evening, while he was working near the property line out behind the old barn, he heard the sound of someone sobbing from the woods just beyond. About fifty feet in, he found little Emma there, trembling, all bloodied from the brambles, and with only one shoe. He gathered her up in his arms and carried her through the woods back to the cottage where her mother was in a panic over her missing daughter.

"Everyone assumed that Emma, who had always been drawn to the woods, had just got lost that day. Funny thing was, after that time, she just about stopped talking. A few words here and there to show that she was not dumb, but that was all. What's more, that shoe she lost in the woods, no one ever could find it. Just disappeared.

"Young John, he was moved by her, and over time, as she grew into a beautiful young lady, he fell in love with her. Though she would never say it, she cared for John too, and would sit with him for hours during the evenings without saying a word, just listening to the bullfrogs and the peepers, watching for the great birds that came to rest in the live oaks.

"Then one evening about seven years ago, John came to visit like usual. As he got close to the cottage, he heard a strange commotion from inside— like someone was moaning. He opened the door and saw a large man on top of the girl. Like I said, John was a strong man. You see, as the stranger began to turn, John grabbed him from behind, bent him backwards violently. Then he just dropped that man, a crumpled heap, to the floor. The girl screamed, and to John's astonishment, this was not Emma; it was her sister Estela, who had come to watch the house while Emma and her mother were away to visit the other sister, Veronica, in New Orleans."

"It turned out that the stranger was hurt real bad—his spine was fractured, and he would never be able to stand upright. He'd need a cane to walk for the rest of his life. It also turned out he was not a stranger, but a married man, which was unbeknown to Estela. And what made everything even worse was that the man was Judge Jackson's nephew—Zachary Jackson. Zach was a good-looking guy, and a crafty businessman who liked his women a little too much and a little too young.

"So when John Lagarde went to trial for attempted murder, Judge Jackson had to recuse himself for obvious reasons. But his influence was felt anyway—the long arm of the law, so to speak—and the newly appointed judge ended up sentencing John to seven years in the pen."

Bobby paused and fixed his eyes on me in such a way as to convey that what he was about to say was to be understood deeply and guarded closely: "John Lagarde was released from prison the day before the Judge was attacked. He is nowhere to be found."

V

I returned to the Whiskey River Landing that evening. Shrimp boats were settling in the docks, the muddy waters roiling softly beneath them. It was Monday and the bar was slow. Jean saw me right away and seemed happy to join me at my table. She would be off duty soon, and judging by the way her eyes danced, it was clear she was open to an invitation.

The cop in me regarded her as a fit young woman, about 5'6", 125 pounds, of mixed bloodline, typically Creole in these parts, with tied-back reddish hair that was probably dyed. The man in me saw her as extremely attractive, magnificently curved, with smooth dark skin, full lips and a laugh that soothed like music. The heart in me, however, was sending out very unsettling messages. This was something out of my realm of experience.

I followed her in my car as we drove south along highway 3177 toward Butte La Rose. She was staying at a stilt house over the bayou. We sat on the deck looking across the marsh, where herons flapped slowly as they settled in the cypresses. As the sun sank down behind the marsh, there was a moment when everything turned deep crimson. Maybe it was the wine, maybe it was her, but I'd never felt such a strong sense of belonging to the here and now as I did that night.

I remember her undressing, lying down beneath me, then hovering over me as I lay there completely disarmed, like I was hypnotized, then transported.

It was a union of two bodies and an out-of-body sensation all at once. It was something like being in flight, in pursuit of a brilliant, beautiful, warm dream, and then getting inside it, and feeling like you have finally come home, only to discover that it is fleeting again, always just out of reach.

It seemed like I was still dreaming when I saw her at the door just before dawn. I heard her whisper as she closed the door, "I will see you again".

VI

The weather report called for a mixture of clouds and sunshine, very humid and windy, with a high temperature of 94 degrees and a 50 percent chance of rain. I arrived that evening at the border of Emma Montaigne's property to discover there was no driveway, no mailbox, no address, no sign. I parked on the side of the street and followed a crude path through the woods that was lined with wild azaleas and witch hazel. Eventually I came to a small clearing where I was halted by a very large and powerful-looking red dog, an unfamiliar breed. I froze there, unsure what to do, until I heard a voice call "Shem! Come!"

The dog returned to its master, and I proceeded to the cottage, in front of which sat a woman with uncombed, untrimmed jet-black wavy hair that flowed all the way down to her lap. Much of her face and bosom were covered by it. She wore a long, white dress cape, and as I approached I could hear the creaking of the wood rocker on which she sat. There was an empty chair across from her. She looked at me with a mix of curiosity and amusement as I sat down.

I explained the purpose of my visit—that I was investigating a crime, and was interviewing all the people in the surrounding area. I sensed she knew this was not quite true. My questions were routine: Where was she on that night? Had she seen or heard anything unusual or strange? Had she seen the Judge or his dog that day or that evening? She just shook her head, and it became clear that she was dismissing me. My last question, however, had an effect: when I asked her if she had heard from John Lagarde, she twitched nervously, then leveled a stare into my eyes that startled me with its familiarity. I could not place it at the time, but its sharp lucidity and gravity seemed to cut to my soul. After a few frozen moments, she released me. "You must leave now," she said plainly.

As I returned to my car, there was a sudden commotion: a van came speeding up the street toward me, then screeched to a halt behind my car. A man jumped out and opened the back where a teenage boy was struggling to hold down something as big as the boy himself that was flapping and flopping desperately under a blanket. In sign language, the man gestured for the boy to get out of the way so he could take over. Seconds later, the man had subdued the creature and, followed by the deaf boy, was carrying it down the path toward Emma's cottage.

What I witnessed I am reluctant to say, only because I am a man of reason, of logic, and a believer in natural law. What I saw betrayed my instincts, and if there was ever a way for me to come to Jesus, it would have started there: beneath the blanket was a full grown bald eagle – a magnificent raptor that had somehow flown head-on into a 150-foot-high fracking rig and got trapped between girder joints near the top.

The deaf boy, who had been marveling at its graceful flight, saw what happened, and when he realized that the great bird was stuck there and struggling to free itself, he climbed the steel ladder up the side of the rig and somehow managed to free the wing and claw that were caught. The Eagle attempted to fly off, but it could not maintain altitude. It descended awkwardly, crashing to the ground below. There the deaf boy and his father subdued it with the blanket, loaded it in the truck, and drove here to Emma's place.

The man set the bird down on top of a massive stump—the remains of a live oak tree. It was surrounded by small pots containing what appeared to be various herbs, leaves, bark, and small animal bones. By now the eagle had stopped struggling, seeming to have given up. Its eyelids shuttered slowly, its broken wing lay limp and twisted and crooked, and two of its talons were bent 90 degrees, nearly broken off. Its beak opened and closed as if gasping for air.

Then it happened: Emma stood over the eagle with her back to us, spreading her white cape with her arms to block our view. She then began chanting in a tongue I did not understand. At first it sounded sad, mournful, almost as if she was crying. Then it took on a rhythmic pulse, and became melodic, lyrical, then joyous—a sound of laughter that seemed so familiar to me. The clearing in which we were gathered was suddenly shrouded within dense, black clouds. There was a peal of thunder, a flash of lightning, and a powerful gust of wind. When the curtain lifted, we saw that the bird was aloft, winging awkwardly first, then gaining strength as it flew away into the purple and orange horizon. Emma was exhausted and collapsed to the ground in a heap under her white cape dress. The deaf boy who had rescued the eagle helped her to her feet and led her back to her cottage.

VII

That was the same day I found the snake in my bathtub. As I entered my motel room, I noticed small drops of water on the carpet. The light switch in the bathroom did not work, leaving only the streetlight from outside and the bedside lamp to guide me as I undressed to take a shower. Perhaps it was divine intervention, perhaps my police instincts, or just plain luck that I noticed the heavy dark form at the bottom of the tub just before I stepped in. It was a full grown cottonmouth. I learned later that this species was widespread in Louisiana, and highly venomous. It was apparent someone had planted it there.

VIII

On Tuesday morning I was called to another meeting with the Judge, who was anxious to hear any news about the case. Neither Bobby nor I offered any information about the snake. Bobby told him that we were still searching the property for any evidence that did not turn up during the initial investigation four months ago, and that we were re-interviewing all the neighbors. Hugh Jackson III was impatient. "Of course you know about John Lagarde being on the loose. What have you done about that? How can such a stupid man get away from you guys? He must be living in the swamp. Why haven't you brought in the hounds?"

Bobby explained that since John went to prison seven years ago, there was nothing remaining that had his scent on it, and therefore the dogs would be of no use, even if they could smell in the water. I interjected that we were pursuing DNA evidence, employing some breakthrough technology. I assured the judge that we had some of the top scientists working on the case. This of course did not satisfy him. He mumbled some apparent insults and threats, then abruptly dismissed us, waving his stub-hand toward the door.

That evening I drove back to the Landing. Jean Blanchet was not there, and the bartender informed me that she called in that morning to say she was sorry, but she had taken a management job in Lafayette. "Too bad," he said. "She was a hard worker. Real smart, too."

I drove to the hut on the bayou, which was abandoned.

I lay in bed back at the motel, disturbed by Jean's abrupt departure. I wondered about this weird case, about these strange characters, and especially about how, in such a short time, I had become so emotionally invested in this remote place. I was a stranger in a strange land; part of me wanted to quit the case, to leave this hot and humid swampland behind, and to erase all the memories. The other part of me felt as if it had entered a new dimension, a sort of accelerated parallel universe, and that to return to the common world would be a regression into the banal. Then as I was about to fall asleep, the awful visions returned—the helpless crying of the of children, the panicking voices of the police, the blood. I dared not go to sleep.

Later that night I heard a rustling sound outside. From the bathroom window I glimpsed again the image of a large, stooped creature disappearing into the dark margins of the woods and alley.

IX

The next day brought more, mostly routine, interviews with the town folk. No one had seen or heard anything, yet just about all of them had something to say about the wild woman in the woods. Some believed in her as a real healer; some thought she was crazy, and still others said she was an evil witch.

Later in the day I visited the family who had brought the eagle to Emma. I learned from the father that Judge Jackson had somehow managed to use the power of eminent domain to seize fifty acres of his property as part of his fracking enterprise. His son was devastated. He had built a treehouse in those woods and had cut a path that led down to a bayou where he loved to fish. All that land was leveled and cleared to make room for the gigantic drills.

I fell asleep early that evening but was awakened again by the dreams. It was after 10:00 pm when I walked into town and found Jacque's Tavern still open. There were several men at the bar, who turned their heads in unison as I entered. I sat alone in a booth, where a woman with a cigarette voice brought me a menu. "Bar menu only after 9:00," she said. "The Reuben is probably your best bet."

I ordered that, along with a draft beer, which was accompanied by a few shots of bar whiskey. None of it was very good, but I managed to self-indulge enough to get Jean out of my mind.

Struggling to maintain composure and balance, I left the bar and began to walk back to the motel. I remember passing the last of the streetlights to where the sidewalk became a dark corridor of magnolia trees. It was then that something hit me hard in the back of my head, stunning me. As I turned, I barely made out the figure of a stooped man smiling maniacally as he continued to pummel me with a stick. I fell to the ground, trying in vain to shield myself from the blows that rained down from above. Just when I thought I would lose consciousness, I heard someone yell, "Drop the cane now, Zach! Drop it now or I'll lock you up for the next six months!"

Bobby Doucet did not arrest Zachary Hughes, the man who had been crushed by John Lagarde. Instead he told him to go home, and in the morning there would be consequences.

While he tended to the wounds on my head, Bobby told me the story of Zachary Hughes. After he was nearly killed in Emma's house during his affair with her sister Estela, Zachary's marriage deteriorated. He went through a messy divorce, and he was never able to get over his infatuation with Estela. It was like he was obsessed with her. In short, he was a lost cause, and maybe a man to be pitied. After all, it is hard to condemn someone who has already been condemned.

I asked if he had any idea why Zach was after me.

For the first time since I met him, Bobby did not seem completely forthright. He hesitated, then replied, "That I don't really know. He hates everyone, especially Northerners. It must have something to do with the investigation.

I'll check into it tomorrow. Meanwhile, I have an idea where John Lagarde might be hiding out, and we need to take a little field trip tonight."

After stopping for coffee at an all-night diner in Jeanerette, we took a dirt road that seemed to go on and on into deeper and denser darkness. The sound of night swamp creatures grew louder, nearly drowning out the car's motor, and I could catch glimpses of bayou as we drove into the wee hours. Finally we came to a hidden driveway leading to a shack situated at the edge of the bayou.

Bobby knocked on the door, there was the sound of bed creaking, and at length a large black man in white underwear opened it. "John," said Bobby. "This is special investigator Paul James. He is a friend of mine. You can trust him."

John Lagarde let out a long, deep sigh before inviting us in. The room, furnished with just a cot and a table and chairs, smelled like kerosene and catfish. We sat at the table in the pale-yellow glow of a lantern. Bobby said, "I want you to tell Paul exactly what you saw that day fifteen years ago. It is important he hears it from you."

John spoke with a heavy Creole accent, and I had to ask several times for him to repeat his recollections of that night. In the end, I understood at least part of what had really happened.

It was sundown, the same day John had discovered seven-year-old Emma lost in the woods. After carrying her home to her mother at the cottage, he returned through the woods. As he approached the barn door, he saw the Judge inside, frantically digging a hole in the dirt floor. It was highly unusual and awkward to see the judge way out here, so John thought it best to stay out of sight. Hiding at the edge of the woods, he watched as the judge took a small object from his pocket, dropped it in the hole, and covered it up with dirt. It wasn't until years later, while he lay on his cot in prison, that John was able to make some sense out of what he had seen. That object could have been the shoe that Emma had lost.

"I knew that I would never be able to get a warrant to search the Judge's barn," said Bobby when John had finished. "So I knew I had to wait, hoping something would turn up at his house while we were digging for evidence on the assault case. The only thing I found that seemed suspicious was a plastic bag filled with baby-dolls hidden under the porch—you know, the ones little girls play dress-up with." He paused, looking straight at John. "If what you saw the judge burying was really Emma's shoe, then you are the only one who knows where it is."

X

So that was the plan. We would sneak John back to town that night. There would be a brief reunion between John and the love of his life, Emma, at the cottage, and then under the cloak of night, John would take a shovel and a flashlight through the woods to Judge Jackson's property. He would enter the old barn, then dig and dig and dig like only a man who has been in prison ever could. We waited at the edge of the woods, listening to the night creatures and resisting their lullaby. It was near dawn when John returned. In his large black hand was a little girl's sneaker, discolored and decomposed badly after decades, but still identifiable as a match for the one Emma's mother had kept for all those years.

Bobby put his career on the line when he went forward with the evidence. He would face something more dangerous than any 250-pound running back. Soon after the allegations against Judge Jackson were made, a team of defense lawyers was brought in from New Orleans. Bobby began to hear noises outside his house at night, and he received several threatening phone calls from anonymous sources. The prosecuting attorney, who came on with much bravado, soon lost his teeth and failed to make a strong argument. The case never even made it to trial, and all Bobby had done was temporarily soil the reputation of the judge. The long arm of the law had once again served the judge. Meanwhile, John was jailed and waiting trial for numerous parole violations. Worse, he would also be charged with the vicious assault on Judge Hugh Jackson III, for which he would face life imprisonment.

XI

However, no matter how long a corrupt arm of the law may be, it still must have fingers with which to clutch its victims and arrest the truth. The hand of justice would prevail after all.

The day after the case was dropped, Judge Jackson and his little band of lawyers walked victoriously up the wide stairway of New Iberia City Hall. At that time the steps were in disrepair—the concrete had cracked along the edges, and pigeons had become a nuisance as they took shelter underneath. As a temporary precautionary measure, PCV pipe hand rails had been placed along the outside edge of the stairs. As Judge Jackson reached one of the last steps at the top of the stairway, a lone pigeon flew out through a crack beneath. As it swerved upward toward his face, the judge was startled and lost his balance. Then, after reaching for the rail that his fingerless hand could not grasp, he tumbled down the steps to his death.

XII

Soon after the accident, I learned that the forensic people had discovered a fingerprint at the scene of the crime in the Judge's yard. This evidence I would keep to myself, for a while at least.

As she promised on that early morning in the stilt hut, Jean would see me again. We met for dinner at the Blue Dog Café. At first I didn't recognize her: her hair was not red, and it was not tied back. It was jet black and long and wavy and beautiful. She wore a striking red cape dress, very much like the white one worn by Emma Montaigne when I met her at her shack in the little woods. As I looked into her magical eyes, the ones that had hypnotized me that night, it all became perfectly clear.

"So, which of the Montaigne sisters are you?" I asked.

"I'm Estela, Estela Jean Montaigne," she sighed. "And I'm sorry that you had to be involved with this mess, especially the part with Zachary Hughes. I hope you can forgive him. His life was destroyed a long time ago."

"You should know that we found fingerprints at the scene," I said. "And I'm pretty sure they won't turn out to be John Lagarde's."

"I'm pretty sure you are right, and I am so glad for John. He is a good man."

"You know that I will do whatever I have to do in order to make sure he goes free."

She paused, then smiled sadly, "Yes. But I'm not worried. There are a few good reasons not to worry. You are a resourceful man, Paul James, and you will do the right thing. Perhaps it will simply be that justice has been served, and this will all end well enough."

"I can't imagine what it would be like to have a twin," I said.

"Twins? Oh no, Mr. James, we are triplets. But I don't think you would want to meet Veronica. She is a very intense and mysterious woman."

Billy Buck and the Bear

I

The pictures of the scene revealed a contorted heap of bloodied flesh lying on a bed of grass and dirt near an electric wire fence. One of the young man's arms was unhinged from his body, and a rifle lay several feet from his outstretched hand. The bottom two wires of the fence were snapped apart at a post. What struck me most, though, was the close-up shot of his face. This young man—who, according to everyone who knew him, had scoffed at the world and was destined to die a violent death—wore an expression of serenity.

II

I came to the small city of Gold Creek in early May as the fitful spring winds were settling into early summer. The morning air was rife with the smell of lilac and the sound of lunatic birds. Huge oak and maple trees lined the streets as I drove through the wealthier residential areas near the college. Children played in the yards, dogs barked at anything and nothing, lawn mowers buzzed in the distance, and it all felt to me like America stood still, fixed in some past era.

However, like most cities and towns in the Great Lakes region of the Northeast, Gold Creek's future lay buried in the past, which was evidenced by the slow but steady exodus of its residents to the warmer prospects of the West and South. Since the 1950's, due to the incremental shutdown of factories, its population had shrunk from 100,000 to just over 50,000. There was nothing to replace the good paying factory jobs, and those who stayed had to accept a lower standard of living. There were now three socioeconomic classes (not counting the college students) in Gold Creek— the nonworking poor, the working lower middle class, and the "professionals"—lawyers, bankers, doctors, college professors, and a handful of wealthy private business owners.

As I turned down Lincoln Street into a working-class neighborhood, it seemed like one out of every three houses was vacant. Gangs of vandals, those rebel stepchildren of the declining economy, had gotten to many of them, spray-painting epithets on walls and breaking windows. The windows were now boarded up, a final muting of the glory days of middle-class working America.

Yet, in stark contrast to all the pop-up cities of modern America, Gold Creek impressed me as a place of some integrity. Despite the economic decline, the downtown architecture had resisted a host of cheap redevelopment ploys and clung tight to its history. The 150-year-old, 3-story brick buildings have stood strong in the face of the decline, with many of the laid-off factory employees now working as up-start masons, carpenters, and jacks-of-all-trades (earning less than half their previous union wage). The three bridges that cross over the meandering creek downtown continue to be repainted every other year, and a percentage of tax money goes to small business in order to upgrade their store fronts. Thus, the city of Gold Creek has remained a place of good enterprise, boasting a small but vibrant downtown.

Eight miles west of Gold Creek loom the Goahonda Mountains, a small but densely forested range consisting of a seldom-visited state park, a hundred or so 10-acre plots of land for sale cheap, and the Wachitah Native American Reservation, population 432. The Reservation consists of mostly one-story, ranch-style homes and trailers scattered along the winding creek and highway

53, the only road through the Native land. As I drove through Wachitah on my way to Gold Creek, the people seemed to gaze listlessly at the road from their porches. It was as if they had assumed a kind of sad resignation after centuries of broken promises and forgotten dreams.

Here were the vestiges of a once-proud tribe, struggling now to navigate the survival bridge between the past and the future. While so many tribal nations across America had prospered through tax exemptions and casino enterprises, the Wachitahs had been largely ignored by US government agencies, mostly because of their isolated location and a lack of business savvy or ambition among the chiefs. Moreover, there was much dissent among them, especially in trying to determine what aspects of their culture should be preserved and what kinds of deals should be brokered with the white people.

They did manage, however, to cut a deal with the US government to provide bus service for the Wachitah children to attend public school in Gold Creek. This, now and historically, has been a thorny proposition. For the Indians, there is the memory of white boarding schools and their "kill the Indian to save the man" philosophy, a period after the Plains Wars when children were physically torn away from their parents, then punished for speaking their native tongues while being force-fed white man's values. Today, for the Gold Creek public schools, there is the challenge of motivating Native children to come down from the mountain and attend school on a regular basis.

On the day I arrived, Gold Creek was more like a muddy river. Heavy spring rains had soaked the Goahonda Mountains, resulting in a swift and powerful confluence of several rills that had swelled the main creek to the brink as it rushed down the escarpment. By the time it reached the level ground of downtown Gold Creek, it was water barely under the bridge on which I stood. It was here I came to investigate the death of Billy Buck.

III

That afternoon I went for a late lunch at Marshall's Diner on Main Street. The waitress, a stout and loquacious woman who seemed to know everyone's business, was happy to provide a description of the goings-on in town, including some frank editorializing about all kinds of issues. I managed to steer the conversation toward the death of Billy Buck, a topic which, for some reason, folks were not inclined to talk much about. Nevertheless, from the waitress and a few other folks at the counter who chimed in, I learned part of his story.

He was not a popular kid in high school. He was a subpar student and had a small circle of friends, mostly lower income kids from broken homes. He was certainly not a bad looking boy; on the contrary, he was described as a Brad Pitt/Robert Redford/James Dean kind of character, with sandy-blond, wavy hair, a strong jaw, dimples, and fiery grey eyes. However, he was cursed with a facial expression that seemed fixed in a perpetual smirk, an appearance that made him seem intimidating to those smaller and younger, yet a target for those older and stronger. They told me that if I wanted to know more, I should go to the Gold Creek Public School administration building and talk to the people in charge.

The Superintendent of Gold Creek Schools, Jane Archer, was eager to share her concern.

Her spikes clacked loudly as she led me into her office. It was easy to see that, despite her lack of facial make-up and tight bun hairstyle, Archer was a very attractive woman in her mid-forties. She walked with a confident swagger that reminded me of someone who was comfortable around horses, and I had a sense she was one who preferred jeans and boots to the tight-fitting skirt she was wearing. As she spoke, it appeared she was pained by the memories, and she still suffered from the guilt of not having done more for that kid.

"I had Billy as a student when he was in 8th grade, and I remember him well. As you might guess, 8th grade is a time when it's hard to separate the kid from the Id. All the wild new urges that come over them, and they don't know how to handle any of it.

"Billy was quiet at first, but as the year went on, he started bullying smaller kids, and at the same time he was getting bullied by athletes and high school boys. He had that look on his face, you know, the kind that invites trouble. I tried to reach out to the family a couple of times, but it was too difficult. The father was drunk most of the time, and the mother seemed to live in a shell. Billy had a sister, but I never had her as a student. People say she was real quiet and stuck close to her mother.

"In high school, Billy was suspended several times for getting in fights, including three especially nasty ones with the same kid—Robert Two Feathers from the Wachitah Reservation. Robert was also a troubled kid—his father was hit and killed by a drunk driver. Like many from the Rez, Robert attended school sporadically and, according to his teachers, grew increasingly bored and frustrated in the classroom.

"The two boys had developed a fierce mutual hatred beginning in 7th grade, and from what the other kids said, they were evenly matched; neither could dominate the other. The last fight, according to the boys who witnessed it, was especially violent.

"It was at the usual spot—the crook in the creek behind the abandoned mill. The boys were in 9th grade. Two Feathers had the advantage that day, having Billy in a choke hold. In desperation, Billy grabbed some rusty old wire cutters that lay on the ground. He stabbed Robert deep in the thigh, causing him to howl in pain. Robert Two Feathers ended up in the hospital with a severe infection. He would walk with a limp for the rest of his life. Neither of them graduated from high school. The saddest thing, Mr. James, is that those boys were so much more alike than they were different. In another life, they might have been best friends."

IV

That evening I went to the College Inn, a local bar that, despite its name, drew a lot more middle-aged residents than college students. It smelled of stale beer, and its walls were decorated with old pictures of local athletes and other high school memorabilia. I learned from the bartender and some folks at the bar that Billy Buck's father, Ray Buck, was a mean drunk. Despite periodic attempts to go straight, he would inevitably fall off the wagon. This was a cycle that would repeat itself over and over again: after a few happy, clowning-around days, the old man would swing to a dark and violent mood. During those episodes, Billy was the near and easy target, and he had the belt buckle scars to prove it.

Ray Buck died from a heart attack while Billy was in the eighth grade, leaving Billy, his younger sister Bonnie and his mother Lola in a house that was paid for (the old man had managed to keep a job at the radiator factory). Lola retreated into a TV-watching stupor to the fill the void that remained in the wake of the storm that was her husband. Bonnie was prone to fits of crying for no apparent reason, if other than to elicit some affection from her mother. Hence, Billy came and went from their Lincoln Street home as he pleased, beholden to no one but himself and his tenuous gang of ne'er-do-wells.

From the bartender at the College Inn, I learned the name and number of someone who knew Ray Buck well.

V

The next morning I met Dan Jamison at the diner. Jamison had been a co-worker and on-and-off friend of Ray Buck. They both had kids about the same age, and the families had taken a few vacations together. Dan paused frequently to clear his smoke-riddled throat as he told me about those summer days at the camp on Lake Erie

As Jamison spoke, I imagined happier times for Ray and his family out there by the water. He drank less, keeping busy working on the cabin or the boat. Perhaps he was entranced by the sounds of the lake—the incessant lapping of waves against the shore, the baby cries of the sea gulls, and the crescendo and decrescendo of the motors of fishing boats as they came and went in the infant and ancient lights of dawn and dusk.

Such was the calm before the storm that would begin on the last day of their last summer trip to the lake.

It was one of those hot and humid evenings in August—the sun, like a dull coin, was hovering just above a lead-grey horizon. Suddenly everything changed. A gathering of black clouds and fierce wind gusts mounted an assault on the shallow waters where Bonnie and Billy played. As Billy felt the powerful undertow that pulled at his hips, his instincts turned him toward shore. He pushed hard against the current to regain the beach. Bonnie, however, was already being pulled inexorably by the back-flow into deeper waters. She was now flailing and screaming as the waves came over her again and again. Billy stood as if frozen, unable to do anything. Suddenly, his father appeared on the rim of rocks above the beach. With incredible speed and purpose, Ray was in the water stroking powerfully toward his daughter, who had now disappeared beneath the surface.

With one last blind plunge, Ray managed to grasp his daughter by her hair and pull her up, back into the wild air. Swimming on his back and riding the waves, Ray brought her to shore where he was able to revive her.

From that day on, Bonnie would unconditionally love her father, who in turn displayed an uncharacteristic, heartfelt tenderness toward her. Later that year, on Bonnie's 10th birthday, Ray went to an elite jewelry store and bought her a very expensive crystal unicorn, a precious little item that Bonnie cherished.

For his birthday a month later, Billy received from his father a voucher for swimming lessons at the local YMCA pool. When he skipped the first lesson to hang out with his friends, Billy received a severe beating, one with an emphatic message about what happens to cowards.

VI

After dropping out of school Billy went to work for a garage where he fixed flat tires, pumped gas and did some general repair work under the lift. An accident with a propane torch while he was burning off a rusted bolt left him with a severely scarred left forearm. After an extended hospital stay, he applied for social security disability benefits, which he began receiving several months later. Thus he was able to work under-the-table at the garage and save up a little money to buy a used car. However, at home his mother and sister grew less and less tolerant of his late-night antics and his shirking of any kind of household responsibility. Since he had already turned 18, they insisted he leave the house. He did so, but not without taking a few valuable items with him, including Bonnie's precious crystal unicorn, which he figured he could sell if the going got tough.

Billy had reckless driving habits. He had already been arrested twice, and he knew that one more incident would result in his loss of license. He realized that his best choice was to rent an apartment downtown, close to the garage where he worked and to the bars where he could walk to meet his friends. The little gang earned a reputation for picking fights with the local college students and bringing the police to bear. This recklessness went on for less than a year before his friends tired of it. Moreover, Billy's neighbors in the apartment building had by now complained enough about his loud music and his general disturbing behavior to have him evicted. He was given a week's notice.

Late that Saturday night, while in an especially ornery state of mind, Billy entered Joe Miller's Bar and Grill near closing time and picked a fight he should not have picked. His target was a short but potent hockey player from Erie, who wasted no time in slamming Billy up against the wall, punching him hard in the face, and kneeing him in the groin. Within seconds, Billy dropped to the floor, bloody and limp. Things may have gotten worse if it were not for Sarah Miller, the bartender, who came between them and ordered the hockey player to leave or she would call the police.

Sarah was Joe Miller's only child, the light of his life and his only reason to carry on after his wife died of cancer two years ago. Sarah was a uniquely pretty girl, with the long, shiny black hair, smooth brown skin and huge black eyes of her Mexican mother, along with the freckles and lean build from her father. She represented the best of both, and the loyal patrons of the bar knew that she was, even at only nineteen years old, fully capable of managing the rough business she had inherited from old Joe, who never fully recovered from his wife's death.

Now, kneeling on the floor, Sarah held Billy's face with firm but gentle hands. Wiping away the blood from his cheeks, she coaxed him back to consciousness. Then, in a kind of epiphany, she saw reflected there in his wild and frightened eyes something like a broken soul. She felt an affinity, as if he had been sent to her. As Billy regained his senses, he too saw something vaguely familiar, something like hope, perhaps. And so she took him upstairs to her apartment and tended to his wounds. For a couple of months there would be tenderness and joy and laughter in both of their lives.

VII

Billy stayed with Sarah and her father through the autumn and into Christmas season with all its downtown gaiety. One might wonder if the two had met in any place other than a bar they could have made it. But even though Billy managed to behave himself most of the time, he was not able to resist the alcohol that came so cheaply, and he became increasingly jealous of the patrons who flirted with Sarah. He also became less tolerant of old Joe, who seemed to grow more senile every day and didn't show much appreciation for Sarah's hard work. Billy began to resent how she doted over the old man.

One night, after he had had too much to drink, Billy suggested that Sarah should sell the bar. They could go in together and buy some cheap property he knew about in the Goahonda mountains.

This was the beginning of a quick end. She would never abandon her father, and the mere mention of it took her to a place in her mind where Billy could not follow. She built an insurmountable wall. At first he pleaded with her. Then he threatened her. And then, after she told him to leave, he took her by the throat and thrust her against the wall. For a moment, as he clenched his fist, the madness seemed so natural, that this was how it must always be, how things would always end up. Yet something stronger held him back, and so he released Sarah and walked away from that bar never to return.

VIII

The following account I was able to piece together from the owner of the garage where Billy worked along with various acquaintances that had business dealings with him over the three months after he left Sarah and Joe's Bar and Grill.

Billy bought twenty acres of mostly wooded land along a small creek in the Goahonda mountains. It came with a large cabin and an acre of cleared land just upstream from the Wachitah reservation. There was an electric line connected from the reservation, but his water was from a well. For a while, all was peaceful; with the help of a constant supply of beer and marijuana, he was able to amuse himself and keep ghosts from the past at bay. He even enjoyed the unexpected company of a stray dog that came upon his cabin, probably a half-coyote refugee. He fed the dog, and the dog listened, at a safe distance, to the silly stories and bad singing of Billy Buck.

Billy commuted to work every day throughout early Spring. He came home one evening to discover that his cabin door had been broken down and his refrigerator ransacked. The place was a mess, with broken eggs and jars and bottles of beer strewn all over his floor. This was obviously the work of a bear who had come away early from its deep slumber and was very hungry, and no doubt, very ornery.

The next day he came home to find his heavy metal garbage can bashed and bludgeoned, and a week's worth of the remains of rotten food lay strewn all over the yard. So Billy went to work securing his cabin. He dead-bolted the door and put bars on his windows. Along the edge of the deck outside, he hung a rope-string of cowbells and pots and pans and other noisy objects. The next day he went to town and bought a rifle at a gun show.

During the evenings now Billy Buck sat on his porch with his gun and his semi-wild dog. He was vigilant, his mind probing the creek and the woods at the edge of his lawn. He would drink and smoke and talk to the dog. As the proper level of inebriation took hold, he would shout into the woods, daring the beast to come forth. A few times he thought he heard rustling through the trees and the sound of deep and impatient snuffling, but the bear did not show itself.

Yet every night, a couple hours after Billy had drunk his way to bed, the dog would yelp. Then there would be a heavy shuffling of feet, then a flurry of noise as the pots and pans and cowbells were set into motion. Sometimes there would be the sound of clawing at the door and shaking of the barred windows. For six evenings, while the days grew longer, Billy sat on his porch with his gun hollering challenges to his nemesis. For six nights in a row Billy barely slept.

On the seventh day, he went to town to the general supply store and bought fifty yards of high voltage, heavy grade electric cable. Over the next two days he set posts in concrete all around the cabin, to which he strung three rows of electric fencing. That evening he resumed his watch, but again nothing appeared before nightfall.

A couple hours later, Billy heard a distinct zapping sound, immediately followed by an alien, guttural cry (it is difficult to imagine the sound of a bear in pain). This happened three times over the course of the next hour, and then silence. Billy finally was able to sleep.

Confident that he had confounded the bear, Billy grew bolder and wilder, much to the annoyance of his neighbors on the reservation. He would spend the evenings shooting his rifle into the woods, or blasting his heavy metal music through giant woofers, and generally enjoying his ability to disturb the peace.

One evening, a tall, black haired woman from the reservation cautiously approached Billy while he was sitting on his porch. She introduced herself as Carrie Two Feathers, then politely asked him if he would turn his music down and stop shooting his gun so much, especially at night. The noise was keeping her family awake, and her daughter rode the early bus to school.

The name struck a chord in Billy—as if some ghost from the past had materialized. He sat silently, as if caught in a dream, ignoring her presence. At length, as the woman was making her way back down the path from which she came, Billy shouted at her, telling her to stay off his property or he'd shoot her.

That night, in the hours just before dawn, Carrie Two Feathers was awakened by the clap of two gunshots. Later that day the buzzards began their circle dance in the sky.

IX

On the morning I was preparing to leave I received a call from Superintendent Archer asking me if I could stop by the school. She wore jeans this time, and her thick brown hair hung in waves down to her shoulders. Her eyes were puffy, and it was apparent that she was very tired.

"There are a couple of things you might want to consider before you close the case," she said. "A few days after the incident, I asked Billy's mother, his sister Bonnie, and Sarah Miller to go with me and the police to look at the cabin—you know, to go through his belongings to see if there was anything they would want to keep or to donate, or if any of them knew of something of value that might have been stolen since the incident.

"The sister, Bonnie, seemed distant, skittish, certainly not much interested in looking around the place. The mother, she just kind of stared into space like she was watching ghosts."

Archer paused, then reached into her desk drawer. In the palm of her hand she held a two-inch crystal figurine of a unicorn, its horn broken. "After Sarah Miller found this in the closet, poor Bonnie and her mom really broke down.

"Also, there is the matter of these." From a plastic bag on her desk, Ms. Archer removed a pair of wire cutters and rubber gloves. The handles on the cutters were old and rusty, but the blades were shiny and sharp. "The police found them in the woods, a hundred feet or so from the fence. They thought you might be interested in them. Oh, and there is also the evidence of several freshly killed fish in the yard strewn along the fence and leading to the cabin door. You know, bears love fish.

"So, I am asking you if there is anything else we can help you with before you leave Gold Creek?"

I thought about this for a long minute, re-imagining what might have happened, and who might have been out there on that night. Finally, I told her that, as far as I was concerned, the investigation was closed. I would report it as a case of, well, man versus nature. In this case, nature won.

"Thank you, Mr. James," she said sadly. "And I was just wondering…do you think it's possible that somehow Billy really met the bear a long, long time ago? I mean, wasn't it always just a matter of time before the bear would finish off the man?"

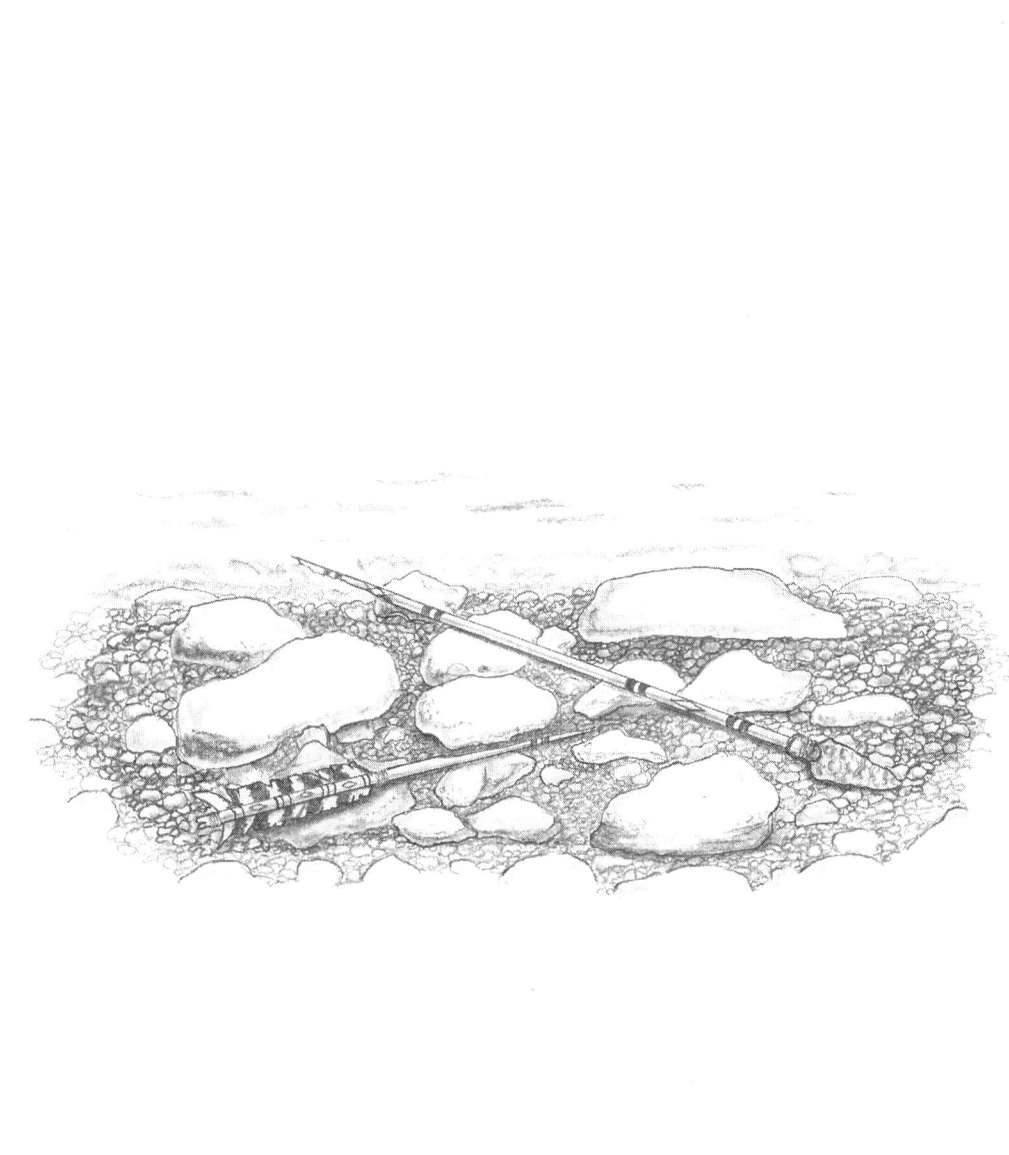

Of Beasts and Giants

According to the legend, the Great Wolf grew angry with humans for killing so many buffalo. The humans would hide in the woods surrounding the herds. Then they would attack fiercely, driving the buffalo into a wild stampede toward the edge of the earth holes where they could not stop in time. Thousands of them fell to their bloody deaths, their bones shattering on the rocky bottom. Then the humans, after taking only a few, left the rest to rot in the earth holes. The vultures came, and then the coyotes, but even they could not consume all the dead buffalo.

But the Great Wolf was powerless against the humans, who were so many, and who had sharp weapons. So he devised a plan to kidnap one of the children. The Great Wolf waited outside the village watching the boys play. One child who had become bored with the games strayed away to explore the woods. The Great Wolf seized him there and took him to the mountains, where he named him Tonkito Lobo, and trained him as a wolf so that he might understand how important it is to take only what one needs and no more. The Great Wolf fed the boy fresh meat, and the boy grew extremely tall and strong. When the boy was a full-grown man, the Great Wolf sent him back to the humans.

There Tonkito took the form of a huge buffalo, twice as big as the others. One day he waited at the edge of the earth hole as the humans came from their hiding places and began to drive a herd stampeding toward him. But before the wild herd came to the edge, Tonkito charged forward. The herd stopped as he rushed by them in the opposite direction, back toward the humans. Then the herd turned and followed Tonkito, running straight at the humans, who scattered into the surrounding woods. After a while, most of the humans came out from hiding to gather on the field near the earth hole. It was there that Tonkito Lobo told the buffalo to turn around again and spread out in a wide line. The herd then rushed at the humans and drove them to their death in the great hole, where the vultures and the coyotes feasted on them.

II

Farreal, Wyoming, population 727, is located ten miles north of Sundance and twenty miles west of Spearhead, South Dakota. It lies at the foot of Bearclaw Mountain, which is part of a neighboring range of the great Black Hills. Farreal is a quiet and sleepy place, especially in February. Most of the residents have homes in the South, where they migrate every fall, leaving behind a flat, white expanse of plains skirting the foothills of the mountain. The only sounds are the whistling of the wind, the choruses of coyotes and wolves, and the zip and zoom of snowmobiles, which are often the sole means of transportation to and from the town.

Most of the approximately one hundred residents of Farreal who stay year-round work either in the village offices and and businesses or at the Talanka Orphanage. The orphanage was established in the late 19th century as an asylum for Native American children whose parents were lost in the Plains Wars. Two decades later, it was converted to an orphanage for children of all races and color. The three-story Victorian brick home, with its adjacent one-story schoolhouse, stands along Farreal's Main Street in the company of several public and commercial buildings, including a hotel and saloon, the general store, an emergency center with a separate office for wildlife management, a tiny post office, and a large storage barn, all wooden structures in the spirit of the Old West. The one irregularity is the Dakota Savings and Loan building, a more modern structure that also houses the Northwest Insurance Agency.

This winter, Farreal was not the usual ghost town. The snowmobile trails had recently been widened to accommodate larger SUV's, the hotel was open for business, and there was considerable coming and going, especially from the Emergency Center and the saloon. A recent series of strange events had brought regional attention to Farreal. There was great interest all across Wyoming and South Dakota. I was sent here by *The Tower* to investigate these strange events. My directives were clear: *Solve this case ASAP, and do not let it gain national attention.*

It was late afternoon and already getting dark when I arrived at the Emergency Center, where I was greeted by Sheriff Sean Peterson, a short, overweight man with thick hands and a round, red face. He introduced me to the three others in the room: police officer Dan Dickerson, who was volunteering from Sundance; Marcia Spence, a reporter for the *Spearhead Spark*; and Noel Oneida, a woman who appeared to be Native American and who worked as a tracker for the County Wildlife Management department.

The Sheriff briefed us on the series of events over the past two months, events that sounded more like a plot from a bad horror film than a real criminal case. A local rancher was up in arms because two of his cows had been killed while in pasture, then dragged off into the front range woods at the base of Whitelaw Creek where they were gutted, the meat and hides taken away. A couple of huskies had gone rogue. There were several reports of a UFO—a greenish dirigible that hovered silently over the mountain before disappearing into the horizon. And then there were the three separate reports of witnesses who claimed to have seen a huge-bodied stranger in or around the town. One sighting was by a group of teenage boys who were partying up along Whitelaw Creek and claimed to have seen it up close—it was at least eight feet tall and carried a bow and arrow. What's more, it had a companion with it. They claimed it was the biggest dog or wolf they'd ever seen, nearly the size of a horse.

"One of the boys gave me a photograph," said Marcia, the reporter. "But it's too blurry, and the images are indistinct. We certainly can't print it without becoming the laughingstock of the county."

"Did the big stranger act aggressive toward the boys?" asked officer Dickerson.

"Apparently not. They say it ran away up the mountain as soon as it saw them," replied the sheriff. "To be honest, this sounds more like a hoax than anything else. But for some people, it's serious business, and if we don't get to the bottom of it soon, we'll have a whole lot of unwanted company, and a lot of them with rifles."

From there the discussion deteriorated into incredible theories about the events, and soon the sheriff grew impatient. "Marcia and Dan, you have a drive ahead of you tonight. We'll get back to this business another day. And Mr. James—I believe you'll need to check in at the hotel. Ms. Noel and I will walk you over and introduce you to Mel. I suspect he's got something cooking for you for supper."

III

Mel was an amiable host. He showed me to my room upstairs on the third floor, noting that there was only one other hotel guest at the moment—a quiet fellow who kept to himself, and claimed to be here to get peace of mind while writing a book. "With all that's buzzing around here lately, I think he's in for a disappointment," said Mel. "And after all the crazy weather lately—record high temperature one day, record low the next—he might get stuck here longer than he expected."

The room was minimally furnished, as to be expected in an old Western town. The wood floor was unlevel. The walls were of rough pine with knots that looked like a hundred eyes staring dumbly. Yet it was clean and surprisingly warm. There was a window overlooking downtown. Mel's hotel and the Talanka Orphanage, the only three-story structures in town, stood four buildings apart, and there was a direct line of vision between them. Through the windows of the orphanage I could see children passing through the halls, probably returning to their rooms after supper. One black-haired young girl stared from her window, her face pressed close, her warm breath forming an imprint that looked like a halo on the cold glass.

Downstairs in the Saloon I ate a generous pot roast dinner and drank a few beers with Mel, who gave me a crash course on the history of the town and its people.

"Like so many western towns, it was talk of gold—mostly made-up stories—that brought the people here. They were looking for another Deadwood – you know, another field of dead trees and a creek full of gold. But no gold was found, or dead trees either for that matter, and nobody really settled here until after the Indian wars. About the turn of the century, some wealthy philanthropists from Rapid City built the asylum here for some of the Indians who suffered terribly in those wars, especially the kids. The idea, I suppose, was to keep them away from the reservations and give them a whole new start up here by the mountains where they could live close to nature while at the same time getting schooled in some of the finer ways of the white man. As you might already know, so much of that "kill the Indian to save the Man" philosophy put out there by the government at the time was a terrible, terrible abuse. But this little school here did some good. While many of the kids would never fully recover from Wounded Knee and other tragedies, some of 'em did, and some went on to become very successful citizens.

"Now Sheriff Sean, he's a good man. He likes his drink, and he gets a little riled up sometimes, especially when tourists come here on their way into the mountains and make a mess, you know, leave their trash, make a lot of noise with their big-wheel trucks and boom boxes, act rude…But his heart is here. He came here as a kid after they opened up the asylum to everyone. His Daddy died in Vietnam, and then his mother got sick. Been here since he was six years old."

I asked him about the tracker, Noel Oneida, the Native woman who never spoke a word at the meeting.

"We call her No. No has been here a long time too. She's deaf and dumb, as they say. But she aint dumb. She reads lips, and especially if you are lying, she reads lips! She's from here too, or I should say she came as a little girl from upstate New York, from one of the Iroquois Nations. She graduated from school a few years after the sheriff, and she never left. She knows the land here like the back of her hand. And man, that girl can ride a snowmobile like nobody's business. If you need to find your way around Bearclaw Mountain, you best ask her."

Later in my room I thought about the tracker named No, and how I would most likely need her assistance in this case. I also thought about her lustrous black hair that reached all the way to the curve of her lower back, and about her smooth skin that belied her age, and her high cheekbones, and her eyes that were large and brilliant and wild as a deer's.

IV
___

The next morning I found Sheriff Sean in the saloon drinking coffee.

"Mr. James," he said, breathing noisily through his red nose. "Mel says you are a man who can be trusted, and Mel always sees the man behind the mask. So I'm gonna fill you in on a couple things I don't want nobody else to know, at least not for now. Can you agree?

"There *is* something out there. Or someone. *No* says she caught a glimpse of a stranger in town a couple weeks ago, over in the alley between the orphanage and the school house. Two nights ago one of the kids at the Talanka Home went missing. As far as we know, she ran away, which happens here often enough. But if word gets out, you know we gonna have a posse ridin' into town from Spearhead and Sundance hunting for Bigfoot, if you know what I mean. Meanwhile, Dr. Cutler, the director of the Tonka Orphanage, has been away on a business trip, but is scheduled to return sometime soon. For the time being, Nurse Smith is covering for us. But when the doc gets back, it will be more difficult to keep this under wraps."

I assured the Sheriff his secrets were safe with me, and that I would conduct my investigation in such a way as to divert public attention from the missing child.

V
___

I was welcomed to the Talanka Orphanage by Sarah Smith, Nurse Practitioner and administrator-in-chief in the absence of the director, Dr. Thomas Cutler. She understood the need for discretion, and she promptly ushered me into the privacy of her office.

Ms. Smith was one of those older individuals whose eyes remained young and daring, always ready to take in something fresh or surprising. I learned from her that the missing child was a Native American girl named Hannah Tremaine. She was nine years old, brought here a couple years ago from a shelter in South Dakota. I also learned that the director of the orphange, Dr. Cutler, lived in Sundance and came to the orphange as little as possible.

"Hannah's father George Tremaine was a pro basketball player for the Dakota Wizards in the NBA D league. His wife had some bad habits, including alcohol and drug abuse, and worse. One night after a loss on the home court, Tremaine came home to find his six-year-old daughter alone in the house. His wife was missing. He tracked her to a local motel room where she was with another man. Tremaine broke down the door and beat both of them very badly. He was arrested and sent to prison.

"So the child was put up for adoption, and soon after that the mother died of a drug overdose. When Tremaine got out of jail, he tried to get custody of Hannah but was denied. Since then nobody's heard from him."

According to the nurse, Hannah was a laconic and introverted child who was not inclined to open up to people, especially adults. However, she had a best friend, Val Johnson, who was very talkative, and I might learn something from her.

As I entered her room on the third floor I recognized right away the dark hair and the dreamy face in the orphanage window across from my room. She was a black-eyed reservation kid whose parents died in a car wreck several years ago. Despite those sad circumstances, Val was a cheerful little girl and eager to talk with me, especially about her friend Hanna.

"I'm not supposed to say anything," said Val with an air of importance. "But I think I know where Hannah went." I told her I was all ears, which seemed to confuse her. She stared at my ears, one of which was missing part of a lobe which had been bitten off during a fight I had in prison. Then she laughed and continued her story.

"She went with the giant, the one she called Tree Man. She always talked about Tree Man. She said he would take her somewhere better. Where we didn't have to do chores and math."

I asked if she had ever seen Tree Man with her own eyes. She looked at me suspiciously, then smiled and said I was silly, because her *own* eyes were the only ones that she could see with...and yes, she saw him once, outside her window—he was so tall he could stand on tip-toes and look in the windows way up here.

"But Hannah was his best friend here, not me," said Val conclusively.

On my way out of the orphanage I noticed the fire escape leading to the third floor.

I also noticed boot prints in the snow, probably from the night before, leading from the back of the orphanage to the schoolhouse.

VI

The meeting that afternoon was in the saloon to facilitate a larger gathering. Mr. Nelson, the banker, was present, along with Mr. Heath, the insurance agent. And there was Nurse Smith, whose lively eyes would not give away her secret knowledge.

Dickerson, the officer from Sundance, was ready to talk. "I think we need to get proactive on this case, Sheriff. I'm not sure what you've been doing around here lately, but I sent one of my boys up the creek, and look what they found in the water near where the cows were slaughtered."

With a latex glove on his hand, Deputy Dickerson held up a broken arrow for all to see. It featured an authentic flint head, hand painted shaft, and bird feathered fletching—clearly the work of a serious craftsman.

There was a murmuring among the group in response to this revelation. Dickens continued. "Now I don't know much about Inspector James here," he said, avoiding eye contact with me. "Don't know who he works for, or where he comes from, but I think it's time we got some real law enforcers here to work this case before we lose more livestock, or worse. You know, a lot of psychopaths start out killing animals, and then move on to...you know what I'm saying."

"Officer Dickerson," said Sheriff Sean, his face reddening as he tried to control his temper, "When you say 'we,' I think you are forgetting that you don't live here. And if finding an arrow in the creek is evidence of some terrible crime, then I'm a full-blooded Comanche."

The banker protested. "Nevertheless, those ranchers are my clients, and for them to lose money is not good for anyone."

"Agreed," said the insurance agent. "And we need to settle this matter ASAP."

Lunch was served at the hotel, where the conversation shifted to the weather. A powerful winter storm was forecast for the next few days, and the sheriff announced that the investigation would be put on hold until it had passed.

It occurred to me then that *No* had disappeared from the meeting before lunch.

VII

That evening a jeep pulled into town and parked by the orphanage. Dr. Cutler, the Talanka director, was returning from a month-long business trip. A short time later, two more vehicles arrived. Four men entered the building. I recognized three: Mr. Nelson from the bank, Mr. Heath from the insurance agency, and Deputy Dickerson. The fourth was a very tall, broad-shouldered man with long black hair. He appeared to be Native American. It was a short meeting, and in less than an hour the four men drove away just in time to avoid the change in weather.

As I sat in my room by the darkened window, strange half-dreams lurked in the margins of my consciousness. It was now after ten o'clock. Just as I was surrendering to the dreams, a light inside the old schoolhouse across the street flickered on and off.

Bitter cold winds swirled among the alleys as I circled behind Main Street to the back of the school. Through a window, I could see in the quivering light of a candle the figure of a person working with quick hands, placing long, bright, pointed objects into a wooden box. As my eyes adjusted, I saw the long black hair and the slender body. It was *No*, and she was carrying a box of arrows down into the basement of the old schoolhouse.

VIII

The storm arrived with a fury, and travel anywhere in or around Farreal was severely limited for the next two days. The other hotel guest emerged from his room occasionally to get his dinner from Mel and take it back to his room. He was not inclined to conversation, even under the dire weather conditions. On the second night of the storm, the sheriff arrived at the saloon, redder than usual from the biting wind outside.

"Mr. James," he said, shaking off the snow as he pulled up a stool at the bar. "I think you may have figured out that as soon as this storm is over, another one is going to start. I'm here because I am fresh out of ideas and looking for help."

I took the opportunity to allow the sheriff to explain what was really bothering him. Then I would determine whether to share with him what I witnessed last night.

The sheriff was ready to drink, and Mel accommodated him generously.

"OK, then," said the Sheriff, trying to sound sober. "Here's the scoop. I learned from sources I choose not to disclose that someone, or some group I should say, has big plans for Farreal. The good banker, the good doctor, and Deputy Dick…Ha, I like that…Deputy Dick, ha…Anyway, those three, along with a rich Indian from Sioux Falls have a plan to turn us into a casino resort town. With all the rumors about some giant Indian out here in the mountains, they think they've got the perfect gimmick. Add the missing girl into the mix, and they've got instant national media attention—everyone will have heard of Farreal, home of the Monster Kidnapper. There was even talk about crossing over into a superhero theme, some sort of Big Moccasin-meets-the Hulk idea. Sickening, isn't it? So, downtown would get a face-lift, you know, the wild west façade thing. The interiors of all the buildings on the boardwalk here would be remodeled for slot machines. The orphanage will be closed, the building condemned or converted to a hotel. There is no plan for what happens to the locals."

He ordered another round of drinks. "As for *No* and the arrows, all I know is that she makes her own for hunting purposes, and she sells some to collectors and at craft shows. As far as the broken one in the creek, I have no idea, and she wouldn't talk. Now I'm getting worried because I haven't seen her in two days. *No* is a proud woman, with a deep soul that is steeped in these mountains."

As the sheriff finished his story the room fell quiet but for the howling outside of the winds whipping the snow across the plains. I saw no need to disclose what I had seen in the schoolhouse at the present time. But I did assure him that I understood the gravity of the situation, and that I would do whatever I could to help save Farreal from being exploited.

As I returned to my room upstairs I was overcome by the feeling that I was displaced, that I had been sucked into a tesseract and transported here to this 19th century saloon. I was an anachronism, out of place and time, without relevance, a hostage in an unreal world. And I felt vulnerable—the dreams were circling the wagons, it seemed, and I had heard nothing from *The Tower*.

IX

In the morning, the sun rose meekly over a frozen tundra. The mountains wore a green-and-white apron of snow and pine trees. Slowly the town showed signs of life, as storekeepers hung open-for-business signs on their doors and shoveled their walkways. Then there was the smell of bacon coming from Mel's kitchen. For a little while longer there would be peace in Farreal.

By ten o'clock everything had changed. First, two snowmobiles arrived almost simultaneously, each carrying a stack of newspapers—one from Spearhead, the other from Sundance. The headline news spread rapidly: GIRL ABDUCTED FROM ORPHANAGE.

An hour later two convoys of snowmobiles roared into town, a half-dozen in each group. Their drivers, armed with weapons ranging from hunting rifles to semiautomatic pistols, gathered in a circle outside the barns. Deputy Dickerson climbed onto the loading dock and, with an air of great self-importance, began to lay out the strategy: form two separate lines starting at the bottom of Whitelaw Creek, then proceed up the mountain, flanking out into the woods on either side of the creek.

I returned to my room hoping desperately to hear something, anything, from *The Tower*. Suddenly there was a knock on my door.

"Mr. James, I have information that I am not supposed to share with anyone, but I think you should know," said Nurse Smith. "When I was asking the kids about Hannah, one little boy said that he saw a very tall man in her room early that morning. I checked the visitors' log and there was no record of any visitors, not for Hannah or anyone else during that entire month. It is concerning because, as I told you earlier, her mother is dead and her father has not reported to his parole officer in North Dakota. Funny thing is that when I told Dr. Cutler about all this, he seemed disinterested, or maybe more like distracted. He told me he would look into it, and that I should not speak of it to anyone until after he made some calls.

"There is something else that has bothered me for a long time. I could never understand what it meant, and there was really no one to share it with, so I just kept it to myself. You see, last winter I was down in the basement of the school looking through all the junk there, just trying to make a plan to get it cleaned out. I came across an old notebook inside a desk. I opened it and found a very strange letter, along with several remarkable little paintings of arrows and buffalo and wolves. It may interest you, and, since I am probably going to lose my job anyway, here it is."

Dear No One

I can't live here anymore. I have out-grown it, like everything else—my clothes, my friends, even my teachers. It is time to go. I am ready for the journey, and with your blessing I know I will be OK. I will see you during the winters ahead, when I may need your help.

Love always,
Maka

"One more thing, Mr. James." said Sarah Smith. "There is a legend here at Talanka about a girl who grew so fast she could no longer fit inside the buildings. The children in the school began to tease and taunt her, so she fled to the mountains and made them her home. However, she returns every winter and brings with her a powerful storm as her revenge."

I knew then who No One must be, and I had an idea about her friend Maka. And I knew they were in danger.

Then at last a message came from *The Tower: There is a second creek. Find No.*

X

The Sheriff sighed deeply when I relayed to him this information. "There was a girl who came here a few years after me, the same time as Noel. She was here only a couple years, but she was kind of famous at the school because her great grandparents were pure Lakota, fought Custer at Little Bighorn. She was real quiet, hardly talked. Then she started to grow, and man did she grow fast—nearly seven feet by the time she started high school. We thought maybe it had something to do with the change in diet here at the school, you know, the government issued nutritional package. After a while, because she was so big, the kids started ganging up on her. This was when I first became Sheriff in this town. I remember the time I got called to the school after she beat the living crap out of three boys who were trying to bully her. According to witnesses, the boys were calling her names, and I heard that they were pretending she was a buffalo and were throwing sticks at her like they were spears. All three boys had to be transported to the hospital in Spearhead. And afterwards she disappeared, never was seen again. I always felt in my gut that *No* knew something about all that."

XI

About three miles west of Farreal and Whitelaw Creek was Cold Spring Brook, which followed a narrower and steeper path up Bearclaw Mountain. Carrying a pair of snowshoes, I rode on the back of Sheriff Sean's snowmobile as he sped up the broad side of the mountain, running more or less parallel to the creek.

After we had crested three hills, he stopped at the edge of a ravine where the snow was deep and the decline to the creek bed steep. Abandoned there at the rim was No's snowmobile. Leading down along a narrow ledge and marking long and even strides were the tracks of her snowshoes.

This was the end of the line for the sheriff, who knew at this point he would only slow me down. He wished me luck as I strapped on the awkward racket-like footwear and set out, gradually gaining speed and confidence as I descended toward the creek. As the afternoon wore on, the sun paled to a grey-white coin, and snow fell gently over the hood of my parka. Eventually I reached the bottom, where Cold Spring Brook babbled beneath its ice cover. I was now in the deep ravine, and above me on either side were rock cliffs rising like fifty-foot walls. The sun had disappeared behind the cliffs, leaving me in a tenuous light.

Leaving the snowshoes behind, I pressed on up the creek, carefully navigating the rocks and the ice under my feet. Soon I had the feeling that I was not alone. I caught a glimpse of something moving with incredible agility on one of the cliffs above me. I pressed forward, pulling myself up over little waterfalls by clutching the branches and roots of saplings. Then I saw it again, this time getting a fuller picture of some animal, larger than a man, leaping from one cliff to the next, then disappearing behind the huge rocks and scrub oaks. Coming to flatter terrain now, I trudged ahead with the thin hope that, as long as the steep walls of the ravine continued, the animal could not get down to the creek bed.

It was now nearly dark there in the upper reaches of Bearclaw Mountain. I had no choice but to keep moving, though I had no idea where I was going. Then all hope seemed to evaporate as I turned a corner to find that the ravine was shallowing out. The cliffs were now no more than twenty feet high, and dropping steadily as I approached what appeared to be a level plain. Here I would be easy prey for whatever was following me.

My last turn brought me to an abrupt end. I stood on the edge of a frozen tarn. But not entirely frozen. In the middle of the lake there were moving chunks of ice, and it occurred to me that, even if I could run away from whatever was following me, there was no place to run. I had come to the end of it all. And maybe, I thought, this is the way it does end for everyone: alone, in the middle of a desolate and forgotten place, ready to meet the beast that devours the body and the soul.

As I stood there looking across the lake, feeling like some sacrificial lamb, I sensed something behind me. I turned to face the most incredible threesome I could ever imagine!A woman, more than seven feet tall and dressed in elk skin and beaver pelt, was standing by a huge grey wolf. And with them, dressed in a sleek blue snowsuit, was *No*, looking fiercely across the lake.

Then there was the sound of men hollering from the distance—the posse had arrived at the other creek source across the tarn, with their guns and lanterns and flashlights, ready to claim their quarry. They had already begun to cross the tarn when another sound came from the sky, and a brilliant light flooded over the lake. Quietly floating directly above us now was a green and gold hovercraft, a blimp-like vessel in the shape of a disc.

"Noel," I cried. "Those are my people up there in that ship. They are good people. You *must* urge your friend to go with them. I promise you she will be safe!"

Noel pointed to the wolf, and I told her yes, the wolf too. She nodded, and then signed to Maka, who looked straight at me and said very simply, "I am tired."

The posse of gun-wielding men slowed as they came closer to the middle of the lake, watching incredulously as the airship lowered a shimmering metallic cage that would lift Maka and her wolf to safety. Fearing the thinning ice, most of the men turned back to shore and into the safety of woods. But a small group of them, led by Deputy Dickerson, continued toward us. "Stop what you are doing at once. You are under arrest," yelled the deputy, pointing his gun at the aircraft.

Just then, the ice began to splinter. Deputy Dick and his men, desperate, turned and began to run back toward the shore. But it was too late. Bearclaw Lake then opened its icy jaws and swallowed the humans and their guns.

XII

After closing the case as accidental death following a wild goose chase up the mountain, I returned to my residence in New England. One splendid April morning, I received a letter from Farreal. It was from *No*, and featured the most exquisite handwriting I had ever seen (I suppose that people with communication deficits in some areas compensate very nicely through other means).

> *Dear Paul James,*
>
> *As you requested, I am writing to update you on life here in Farreal in the aftermath of our adventure in the mountains.*
>
> *With great sorrow, I must inform you that Sheriff Sean has passed away. It was sudden, and I don't think he suffered much after his snowmobile crashed off a bridge during a spring storm. He had been ill; perhaps this was a better way for him to go. And, as he wished, I am now the sheriff of Farreal.*
>
> *As for Hannah, her father—George "Tree Man" Tremaine, former center for the Dakota Wizards—was caught taking her across the Dakota border. He did not resist arrest, and has been placed in an NBA sponsored trauma and substance abuse recovery program. It turned out that George had been duped into thinking his daughter was being abused at the orphanage, which led to his taking her away from there. But things are better now, and there is even hope that after his probation he could be given visitation rights. As you know, Hannah loves her "Tree Man."*
>
> *Luckily for us, efforts to build a casino faltered after the events on the mountain. It turned out that one of investors, the Indian from Sioux Falls, was a cousin of George Tremain. When he learned of the scheme and how his cousin and his niece were used as pawns, he scuttled the whole plan. Dr. Cutler moved to Florida in a hurry, and Mr. Nelson took a bank teller position in Spearhead.*
>
> *Of course there is great discussion about what really happened that day at Bearclaw Lake. The remains of the bodies of Deputy Dickerson and his cronies were not recovered until late spring when*

the ice had melted. The surviving posse members, to a man, claim to have seen the giant and the wolf transported by a spaceship. Maybe if one of them had thought to bring a camera instead of a gun, there might have been some evidence.

So, Mr. James, I hope you will come visit Farreal someday. I must tell you that, although I cannot hear or speak, I can see things others can't. I saw reflected in your eyes a dark and troubled soul, one that has witnessed terrible things. Maybe someday you can come and talk to me about it. I happen to be an excellent lip reader!

Love,
No One

The Edge of Faith

How many reasons could there be for a man to fall to his death from a high cliff?

It might have been a pure accident, brought on by a quirk of nature. An unfortunate turn of events may have led him to some precipice at a bad time—like a sudden rainstorm causing him to run for cover over a path that has been abruptly washed away. Perhaps he was a victim of a landslide from a higher elevation, to be swept over the edge and buried alive in the gulch below. Or, on a smaller scale, he might have encountered a snake or a rabid animal which, in its blind madness, lunged at him from the hidden margins of the path, sending him off his charted course and into the deep.

Such a tragedy also might be attributed to human error—for example, a mountain climber pays the price for the malfunction of a rappelling device or crampon. Perhaps it is something as simple as a protruding rock on the path that catches the toe of his shoe, throwing him just enough off balance so that he, despite the last desperate grasping for any solid piece of this earth, passes over the edge empty handed.

More compelling is the notion of the intentional act of one man upon another. There are places in the souls of men where the light of goodness has been extinguished, where conscience has been eradicated, and where any act of evil can be easily rationalized: the strong and opportunistic survive in nature. Murder is as old as Cain and Able. War is inevitable, and competitive killing is an evolutionary act, part of the natural process. Up here in the thin air, it is an easy task: position yourself on the inside of the path, wait for the right moment when the slightest push on the hip or shoulder will send your unsuspecting victim down so rapidly that it is all over in seconds, and the sharp and unforgiving rocks below will have done the brunt of the dirty work as you walk away wiping your hands.

Most terrible of all is the self-inflicted fall—suicide: it might stem from a feeling of being so small and insignificant that one's life has no meaning, and the suffering so outweighs the joy that there is no point in living. In another mind, it might be lunatic whisperings begging for peace and reason, now gathering together to form one clarion voice that peals across the valley to the deaf mountain walls, then returns in a shattered echo that mocks the sender. Or there is the broken and defiant one who, with so little to hold on to and even less to lose, scoffs at the very idea of God and has dared himself so many times, always edging just a little bit closer, until he finds comfort and familiarity there at the threshold. It is no longer a matter of spitting in the face of God, but of the simple resolve to just let go.

But maybe there is one more reason that goes beyond all these.

II

The agency sent me to Maui to investigate what is officially a missing person case, but one that local police assume to be suicide or murder. The only witnesses were the four members of a family of tourists—parents in the front seat, a young son and daughter in the back. The father was driving on Highway 30 along the sharp switchbacks that line the cliffs high above the ocean. Just northeast of Kapalua, they passed a car parked at a scenic lookout point. According to the father and son, a dark skinned, thin man dressed in what looked like a white hoodie was standing at the edge of the cliff looking out to sea and waving his arms. The mother, frightened of the steep cliffs and narrow road, was looking down and saw nothing. The daughter, despite being dismissed by the others, persisted in her belief that there were two people, a man and a woman. The woman was dressed in a white gown. Both son and daughter remember turning in their seats to look back after passing the lookout point. The man, who seemed to have grown taller, leaped high into the air, then disappeared.

They reported the incident to 911, and the police arrived an hour later. The car was registered to a John Hawking of 724 Mill Street, Lahaina. Possible evidence gathered by the police included the prints of a bare-footed man near the edge, some pieces of light-weight fabric, a six-inch piece of ¾ inch PVC pipe, and a small anemometer. The only evidence that might corroborate the little girl's account was a traditional Hawaiian woman's headdress that had drifted into the bushes across the road. Remarkably, the white flowers had not wilted.

Hawking's car was impounded, and the Coast Guard was called in to search the rocky beach three hundred feet below the precipice. After two days, the search was called off; there was no body to be found.

As I stood there at the spot where John Hawking had presumably leapt, it seemed impossible that anyone could survive such a fall. Despite the sheerness of the cliff at that lookout point, it would have required near superhuman strength to leap far enough out to reach the water, and even if he had cleared the cliff, he would have landed among a platoon of jagged rocks that defended the cliffs against the onslaught of the massive Pacific waves.

III

John Hawking lived in a small, barely furnished apartment just a few blocks from Lahaina Water Sports Emporium, less than a mile from the downtown business district. In the bedroom was a single photograph of Hawking and a woman posing at the beach in their swimsuits. This was a remarkably beautiful couple. Hawking was muscular, brown skinned, with wavy dark hair that came to his shoulders. The woman was likely of Polynesian descent, with dark creamy skin, and black, waist-length hair streaked with caramel. She appeared to be athletic, yet very feminine at the same time. She was wearing a Haku Lei of white gardenias.

I learned a great deal about John Hawking from his boss at the Emporium, who had known of him back in high school in Honolulu. Hawking was a state champion swimmer and diver who had been offered scholarships to several colleges, including UCLA. During his senior year, he got involved with a local gang and ended up getting arrested for drug possession. Hawking's father used his influence to get the charges dropped, but the boy grew distant and lost interest in sports.

John Hawking's father was a retired Air Force pilot and Viet Nam War veteran from Louisiana who had married a young woman from the Philippines. Neither parent was forgiving of their son's transgression. Their solution to his troubling behavior was to pressure him into joining the military, a move that effectively turned his life around.

IV

Hawking served four years in the US Army, deploying three times to Iraq and earning a Bronze Star with Valor for saving the lives of a dozen or more soldiers. However, if you asked John Hawking, he'd tell you that was luckier than he was heroic.

It was at the end of one long, hot, and tedious day of a convoy mission when John and his crew got permission to stop their Hummer on the side of the road to take a piss. As the sun settled over the sea of red sand, the convoy continued at a slow pace, which would allow John's crew to catch up after the quick stop. As he was unzipping, John noticed something moving up ahead where the meandering road switched back in his direction. He watched as a figure emerged from behind a garbage pile along the ditch. It crawled out into the middle of the road, deposited a square container, then crawled back across the ditch and disappeared into the margins. The lead truck of the convoy kept going forward, and John suddenly realized that it was heading straight for an IED. Pissing all over himself, John sprinted ahead and managed to flag down the truck just in time. There was a relatively small explosion, but John took some shrapnel in the arm, along with some damage to his left ear drum.

After the war he returned to Honolulu, but his war experience had unnerved him to the point where he was ill-at-ease with all the commotion of the city. So he moved to Maui, got a job as a maintenance worker at the Lahaina Water Sport Emporium, and took up kitesurfing on his own as a hobby. A natural athlete, he excelled at the sport and might have competed at a high level, but he had no heart for that. It was enough just to be out there, at one with the wind and the sea.

One day, while he surfed alone far off the coast, a powerful gust of wind caused him to become tangled in his line. He nearly drowned as he tried to extricate himself from the ropes, the kite collapsing over him. A fisherman came to his rescue, cutting the ropes and pulling him into the boat. John was taken to the emergency room, where he was tended to by Angela Juneau, a beautiful, young part-time nurse and semi-professional hula dancer. He fell in love, she fell in love, and a month later they were married.

V

However, it was not destined to be a lasting union. Angela Juneau worked for a dancing troupe that performed in some of the highest circles on the islands. They were sometimes flown to Honolulu to perform at corporate events. Although John admired his wife's talent and respected her right to perform and to earn money, he became increasingly uneasy about her being away. And though he trusted her, he began to obsess over the idea of her being ogled by the greedy and lustful business executives.

Less than two years into their marriage, there was an accident. It was on one of the trips to the main island that the Cessna 208 carrying Angela and her troupe went off course during a storm. According to ATC records, the plane crashed against a cliff, burst into flames and plunged into the ocean. There were no survivors, and all the bodies were lost to the sea.

At the funeral, John was a broken man, and afterwards the people who knew him became worried as he isolated himself within the walls of his sorrow. However, after a few months, John showed signs of recovery. He returned to work at the Emporium and began attending church regularly at Maria Lanakila

Catholic Church on Sundays, where he passed the offerings basket and occasionally helped Father Tony with the offering of wine at Communion.

Despite his apparent emotional recovery, there was concern by those who knew him over his extreme weight loss and his reclusiveness—John's public life was entirely confined to work and church. Rumors emerged, first that he was sick, and then that John had led some secret life—perhaps there was another woman, or even another man, someone either new in his life or who had been there prior to the accident. (Such banal musings often serve to fill the void felt by those whose belief in love runs shallow.)

VI

I decided to visit the Maria Lanakila Catholic Church and speak with Father Tony, who welcomed me warmly and invited me into the rectory for a glass of wine.

"Yes, John and I were very close friends, despite having many differences regarding our relationship with God. I can tell you that he loved his wife deeply. After the accident. I, like many others, worried about him. He'd lost so much weight, was practically skin and bone. Then not long ago he began to come to church almost every day, praying alone and lighting candles. But you know, he seemed in good spirits, even up to the last time I saw him, which was the day before he went missing. Neither I nor anyone else had any idea what he was planning. You see, even though John and I disagreed on many issues regarding the church, I can say with certainty that he was a highly spiritual man."

I sensed that there was something he was not telling me.

"Mr. James," he sighed, "what John shared with me in confession is not to be revealed. It is my sacred duty to not betray God's trust. But what I can tell you is that somewhere in the warehouse behind the Emporium there is a locked room where John spent a great deal of time. He rented the space from his boss after Angela disappeared. If there is anything that can help you in your endeavor to make sense of his fate, it would be in that room. All I ask is that you be very, very careful about explaining what you discover; on this island, which was once home to pagans and demagogues and mystics and all kinds of story tellers, the Catholic Church still struggles to maintain its foundation of one God and one Son of God. There are those of wavering faith who have a thirst for a kind of magic that is not part of our doctrine."

VII

Outside my window, the sun listed, a red medallion half submerged in the swelling blue waters. I tried to imagine Captain Cook as he sailed into these far reaches of the world during his time—how he first laid eyes on these brown, smooth-skinned people with their shiny black hair. And I wondered how the natives must have perceived him and his magnificent ship as it sailed into their shores, as if sent from the gods.

It was nearly dark when I arrived at the Emporium, which was just closing shop. John's boss was at first reluctant to give me the key, as if whatever was in there should remain locked up and undisturbed. He told me he always had an eerie feeling about that place, and he was worried about how many hours John spent there. But he acknowledged that it was time to move on and get the place cleared out, for better or worse.

As I entered the room I was met with the strong smell of glue, which is common in areas of boat repair. Through the dim light of a single bulb hanging overhead, I could see along the far wall the jagged forms of what appeared to be two pieces of furniture covered with sheets. The room seemed filled with a ghostly silence as I approached shrouded forms.

Removing the sheets of the smaller piece, I discovered a sewing machine. Next to the machine were several small bottles of liquid, spools of wire, needles and thread, and a scrap of light weight plastic material, apparently the kind used for hang-gliders and kites.

Under the other sheet was a large drafting table on which sat a candelabrum. Lighting the three candles, I could see a row of pictures along the wall of airplanes, gliders, kites, and magnificent birds of prey. On the table were various objects, including several long pieces of ¾ inch PVC pipe and a science book titled *Avian Anatomy*. As I cleared away the cluttered objects, I saw the last and most critical piece of evidence: a full-scale model printout of the wing structure of a mature Great White Heron.

VIII

The next morning, I summoned the Coast Guard to take me out along the shoreline of Honokohau Bay to the area beneath the lookout from which John Hawking had jumped. We scheduled for that evening, despite the call for rain, wind, and choppy waters.

When I arrived, the captain told me that it was really no use; too much time had elapsed, and any remains of a body would have either washed ashore miles to the east or been devoured by fish long ago. Despite his resistance, I was intent on finding whatever I could find, and we set out on the troubled waters, dwarfed beneath the hulking shoulders of the mighty cliffs. Wind and waves battered the sides of the rescue boat, rocking it back and forth and causing it to list toward the shore. The captain frowned stoically.

But then everything changed. A half-moon flickered from behind swift moving clouds, and a silver twilight surrounded us as we approached the cove beneath the lookout, the waters quieting as if in anticipation. The captain slowed his engines, steering us closer to the walls of the cliff. Quietly, cautiously we entered into a half-ring of boulders, their opaque faces gazing blindly skyward. And then I saw it: trapped between two rocks amid the slosh and foam was a sealed plastic bag containing a rectangular object that appeared to be a book!

IX

The skies cleared on the way back to the Coast Guard station. If not for the hum of the motor, I might have believed we were sailing high above the waters, still rising, surrounded by the stars, sailing on and on, a new world before us.

By the light of the boat's cabin, I unwrapped the package. Somehow this old leather-bound copy of a Bible had survived the fall. I opened to a page that had been bookmarked and highlighted:

He mounted the cherubim and flew; he soared on the wings of the wind. Psalm 18:10

On that same page was a folded up, handwritten letter:

Dearest Angela,

I have never missed you because I have never really felt that you are gone. I close my eyes and I see you there in front of me. You are alive. Your eyes see. Your lips speak. Your body moves like the waves of the ocean. You are still warm and young and beautiful. Though I cannot embrace you now, I know that there will be a day, a glorious day, when I will hold you again in my arms and nothing in the universe will ever let us part. You are my great and only love. I am filled with faith and joy knowing that, through the miracle of God's grace and beauty, we will meet on that threshold where, without fear or misgiving, I will leap into the sky, our wings will join together, and we will fly away into those heavens that are eternally ours.

Your Husband,
John

Geronimo High

Using the counterfeit credentials provided by *The Tower*, I managed to get hired by Geronimo Central School District as a high school counselor. The job required a week of orientation at the end of the summer break, during which time I often felt exposed as one with little experience working in an educational system. Principal Jack Davis, a tall man with a hawkish face and stiff carriage, had his eye on me. I wondered if this was because he could see me for the imposter I was, or because there was someone else he had wanted for the position but was overruled by the school board. However, despite his skepticism and the tedious training program, I learned the basic requirements of the job and gained a sense of what these kids in this lower socioeconomic community were like. For my office décor, I chose wall posters without corny, inspirational messages, but rather with artistic beauty that could stand alone.

Geronimo High School, a sprawling adobe-type structure several miles south of Taos, New Mexico, served mostly rural families, many of them Mexican ranchers and farmers from the greener plains near the Rio Grande River. There also were kids from Taos whose parents worked in the restaurants or gift shops there, along with a few well-to-do kids who had transferred from the city's wealthier districts for various reasons. Until recently, Geronimo had been a quiet and quaint educational setting with a focus on English as a Second

Language as the foundation of all curriculum. There was a common under-standing that if these children of immigrants were to get beyond a life of ag-riculture or manual labor, they would need to assimilate.

The Tower sent me here because some teenagers were missing. It is not unusual in Mexican American agricultural communities for students to have lousy attendance records—these kids are an important part of the family en-terprise, both as workers and liaisons who travel between their families here and *los Abuelos* south of the border. And beyond that, it is often difficult to get parents to talk about anything other than their work, as they are wary of the agents from Immigration and Customs Enforcement (ICE). Recent events, however, suggested that something more serious was going on in the region, and, according to *The Tower*, it was my job to find out what. Given the fact that I speak little Spanish, I had to wonder if I was the right person for the job.

II

Stationed behind the counter in the front office of Geronimo High was Mon-ica Simmons, a woman whose formal attire and pageboy bob hair style sug-gested a no-nonsense attitude. It was her job to greet people in as pleasant a manner as can be mustered in the face of unpredictable parents. Her smile and general demeanor were business-like and, when need be, calmly dismissive, a style that she had perfected over the years of being on the front lines.

Behind Ms. Simmons was the important office of Principal Davis, which had a large window with blinds that were drawn shut most of the time. On the opposite end of the room was a smaller office with open windows. This was occupied by school security officer Bill Ferry, a former star football player in Taos County. Now, at forty-two years old, Ferry was still a prime physical spe-cimen, and the kids respected that. His wavy blond hair, baby blue eyes, and engaging smile also served him well in his side business as owner and operator of a whitewater rafting outfit on the Rio Grande.

Down the hall and across from the auditorium was the maintenance room, which was not much more than a deep closet for mops and buckets with a small desk and chair facing the far wall. This was a place of refuge for June Maris, the school maintenance person, who was born with a short left arm and leg, along with crossed eyes and just one good ear (the other a skin flap like a mushroom surrounding a small hole on the side of her head). Such deformities affected her carriage, causing her to move in a lurching and crab-like manner. Ms. Maris, who had received abuse from kids and unkind adults throughout her life, found ways to feel invisible. She appeared to be oblivious to her surroundings as she went about the business of mopping floors and cleaning toilets.

I shared the adjacent corridor with two other counselors and the attendance officer. Counselor Carla Adler had been there for thirty years and seemed to know all the short cuts. She closed her door during meetings with students, and those meetings generally lasted just a few minutes.

Joe Sanchez was a middle aged Mexican American. He sported a long, black, braided ponytail, which gave him an air of youthfulness and indigenous mystique. Though friendlier in his dealings with the kids than Carla, he was equally efficient in taking care of business. The attendance officer, Anita Miller, was barely tall enough to see over the counter. She was a loquacious young woman; when she was not talking to a student or staff member, she was on the phone speaking very rapid Spanish to her friends or family.

Our business with the students was largely a matter of scheduling classes to keep them on track for a diploma, which would supposedly ensure their progress toward higher education and a career. I quickly learned some harsh realities about public school administration and the government branches that steer them. There was a huge divide between the philosophical agendas of the education system and the everyday lives of the common people.

Nevertheless, it seemed to me the most important aspect of this job was getting to know the kids personally. This was especially hard to do here in Mexican America. The language barrier aside, they had inherited their parents' paranoia regarding the insecure legal status of so many of their close relatives and friends. There is always the suspicion that we are prying not because we care, but because we are trying to bust someone.

Such were the preconditions as I began to interview students at Geronimo High. Most meetings were routine matters of scheduling the required classes along with electives to keep students busy and not loitering in the halls and cafeteria. In rare instances, we were asked to probe matters of excessive absences, chronic class disruptions, and other behavior issues that security officer Bill Ferry and his discipline team had been unsuccessful addressing. Despite my limited ability to communicate in Spanish, I managed to guide students according to protocol. Over the next few weeks, as I became more familiar with the curriculum and graduation requirements, I also learned to detect the attitudes and emotional vicissitudes of individual students.

III

"So, Mr. James, what's up with Maria Salvador. You got her figured out yet?" asked Joe Sanchez as he, Carla Adler, and I met for our Friday afternoon counselors meeting. "I tell you, man, she's been around the block here a few times, right, Carla?"

I wondered if Carla, with her large black eyes, soft skin, and plump figure was pretty when she was young; it seemed that after so many years at this desk job she had become part of the chair in which she sat, a toad-like queen, barely moving or blinking. She groaned, "It'll be a miracle if she ever graduates."

Sanchez, dressed and ready for the weekend in his flashy Native American poncho and designer jeans, continued. "Sad story, that one. She just seems to want to make problems for herself and everyone else. I tried to reach out to her all last year, but she put up a solid wall. Now she's getting in fights every other day. But you know they can't expel her without going through a ton of paperwork. Not unless she gets caught with drugs, anyway. That would be automatic expulsion."

"The reality is," croaked Carla stirring in her chair, "that the girl is a carbon copy of her older sister, who was nothing but a pain in everyone's ass here. She was on drugs, was dealing them right here at school. And all the drama! It was like every other day she was going to kill herself or someone else. Thank God we got rid of her."

The topic seemed to make Joe Sanchez restless. He fidgeted in his chair, then redirected his gaze to the window when I asked what became of the sister.

"Nobody knows what happened to her, except maybe Maria," said Carla. "Those girls made up their minds a long time ago that school was not for them.

They had an appetite for the wild side. Anyway, the way things have been going lately, we won't have Maria around much longer either."

At the time I wanted to say something about reaching out to those girls, about trying to do something to help them. But given the present mood and company, such a declaration might make me appear naïve or gullible. And maybe they'd be right.

My interview with Maria Salvador earlier that day had been an exercise in futility. She sat slumped in the chair across from my desk in her rainbow spandex pants and tank top, legs crossed, smacking her gum and humming softly while she contemplated her painted nails. Her shiny black hair partially concealed a very pretty face.

Maria ignored my compliment regarding the exquisite tattoo on her left arm—a golden eagle atop a cactus holding a snake in its talons (the coat-of-arms on the Mexican flag). Her responses to my questions were curt or circumventing, though she did offer her opinion that the kids at Geronimo are assholes, and the teachers don't care, except for maybe one—her English teacher, Miss Leslie, was not as bad as the rest.

For the most part, I was invisible—just another adult who doesn't get it. Yet there were moments when I sensed something more—the way she glanced toward the window, or shifted in her seat, or focused her eyes directly on me for a split second seeming to read my mind. It occurred to me that this was a 16-year-old girl who had been to the dark side, and I would need to know what she knows.

That night I received a message from the agency stating that it was their belief that several girls in Taos County could be in danger. I was to guard my cover very carefully as I proceeded with the investigation.

IV

School Security Officer Bill Ferry was in Principal Davis' office when I arrived Monday morning. They were having what appeared to be a very serious discussion, and upon seeing me, Mr. Davis closed the door and drew the blinds. Monica sat at her desk, straightening the items surrounding her computer, and

June, the janitor, was in the hallway getting ready to retreat into her closet as the school buses arrived.

Maria Salvador did not come to school that day, nor the next. On Tuesday afternoon, I requested a personal day for Wednesday, which Principal Davis granted, but not without a look that seemed to express suspicion regarding my intent.

School counselors have access to a good amount of confidential information, so I took advantage of it. The Salvador family lived a few miles southwest of Taos in an agricultural region not far from the Rio Grande. There were four listed residents—Maria, her father Carlos, mother Anna, and a niece Carlita with the same last name. The father was employed at a large greenhouse in that area. There was also contact information for an older brother, Juan, who worked on a pepper farm in the valley near the river.

When I arrived at the Salvador home, there were several children kicking a soccer ball in front of the trailer. As if trained in this matter, they gathered together, then disappeared into the back yard. Mrs. Salvador appeared nervous as I approached. Her English was almost as bad as my Spanish, but I managed to communicate that I was not from ICE, and she seemed to relax a bit. She claimed that she thought Maria was at school, and she frowned darkly when I told her that Maria had been absent all week. She gestured to the smoke coming from her kitchen, abruptly dismissing me so she could finish her cooking. As I pulled away, the children peeked from around the corner, and in my rearview mirror I could see them resuming their game of soccer.

The River Greenhouse was an expansive series of plastic, tent-like frameworks with insect mesh perimeters. There was a constant hum of the evaporator machines and fans that kept the air moist and the temperature low enough so the plants did not burn under the intense New Mexico sun. I found Mr. Salvador in one of the larger houses at the base of a large mesa. He seemed tired, not healthy, and he was certainly uncomfortable with my questioning, opting repeatedly for "no comprendo". I learned very little from him before a young white man, less than half Mr. Salvador's age, hollered something from the gate about getting back to work. Mr. Salvador obeyed, abruptly ending our conversation. The young man who had hollered watched me intently as I exited the greenhouse.

A few miles north on the opposite side of the road was the Esperanza pepper farm. Following directions from a man at the storage shed, I found Juan Salvador with a small group of men toiling in a field of knee-high plants under the high sun near the banks of the Rio Grande. Juan was leaning against a hoe as I approached. He wore a wide-brimmed hat that shaded his dark skinned, boyish face. His sleeveless shirt revealed thin but muscular arms gleaming with sweat and sunscreen. "What can I do for you?" he said in plain English.

After I mentioned his sister's name, he led me to a small pavilion, a respite from the sun where the workers took their breaks. Juan was relieved to learn that I was not from ICE and that I worked at the school. He was proud of having graduated from Geronimo High, where he had been an all-New Mexico soccer player. He explained that, even though he had college scholarship offers, his father was not well, and that his family would always come first.

I asked about his sister Alana.

"Alana, she is dead to me. She got in with drug dealers, and then she left home without saying anything. Our mother had to quit her job at the nursery to take care of the little ones at home. And now Maria—she was such a good kid, so curious and smart. Now she is acting like Alana did when she got in trouble."

When I asked him if he had any idea who these drug people were, he appeared unsettled. "There are things we can't talk about here without risking everything. I will try to get Maria back to school tomorrow. But now I need to get back to the peppers."

V

Juan was successful in his efforts, as Maria returned to school on Thursday. I called her into my office after lunch, and her disposition and dress were remarkably changed from the previous week. She sat up straight and looked me in the eye, waiting for me to initiate. I closed the door.

"Maria, as you probably know, I visited your family yesterday. In my estimation, your parents don't know what is going on with either you or your sister. Your brother has some understanding of the problem, but he feels helpless to do anything about it. Therefore, my concern is not about what's going on at this school, but what is going on somewhere else, and I hope you can believe I am here to help you and your family. Now what can you tell me to help me help you?"

"Nothing more than what my brother told you. Except that for me it's not drugs. I don't do drugs. My brother would kill me if I did."

Maria excused herself and left the session abruptly, leaving me with little more than the satisfaction of having broken down one line of defense. It wasn't until later in the day that I noticed a business card on the floor under the chair where she was sitting during our meeting. It was for *The Rio Connection—Great Golf, Great Spirits, Great Company*. There was a picture of a martini glass, on top of which was the cartoon-like figure of a sexy woman golfer teeing off. The number—308-269-6996—struck me as familiar, but I could not place it at the time.

After school, Joe Sanchez informed me that some of the faculty would be getting together that evening at the Ortega Grill in Taos, and that I was invited. I agreed to join them despite my apprehensions about these kinds of social affairs, especially ones during which there is likely to be a great deal of gossip and complaint, along with some adolescent-flavored silliness. I prepped myself with a couple glasses of wine at my apartment before venturing into the heart of the Taos business district, where actual remnants of the great old American West mingled with the banal commercial businesses of modern America.

The Ortega Grill was an upscale Mexican restaurant with a casual atmosphere in the bar area. Standing by the bar was Miss Linda Leslie, a very pretty, young English teacher who, in the school setting, maintained a conservatively professional appearance—knee-length dresses, her hair up in a bun. Tonight, however, she wore heels, a short black skirt and an emerald green tube top, her auburn hair falling in waves upon bare, tanned shoulders as she drank martinis with a couple of colleagues. Her friends giggled as she cast not-so-furtive glances my way, and I could not help but feel flattered by such a good-looking young woman, despite the juvenile nature of the flirting.

I sat at a table with Joe Sanchez and Bill Ferry. Ferry was wearing a tight-fitting Eddie Bauer polo shirt that revealed his chiseled physique, and he seemed to flex his bicep just a bit every time he raised his bottle of lite beer.

Principal Davis was not present—apparently, it was taboo for administrators to socialize with staff in public settings.

At the table, I told Bill and Joe about my meeting with Maria. Both seemed keenly interested, yet skeptical of Maria's claim of not being involved with drugs. My suggestion that maybe something other than drugs was going on here elicited an impatient response from Bill Ferry.

"Paul, this isn't the big city here," he said, as if incredulous. "We don't have the kinds of problems like down in Albuquerque. And if the thing you're getting at was going on around these parts, you're damn sure I would know about it." Then his tone softened. "You take care of those kids who deserve your help, the ones that want to graduate and move on to better things in life. Leave the others to me and the local police."

The discussion was interrupted as Joe's phone lit up on the table. He excused himself, hurrying off to a quieter spot in the restaurant. Meanwhile, the English teacher in the short skirt was getting quite tipsy. She pointed directly at me, then curled her forefinger, summoning me toward the bar, where her friends were exhibiting the kind of behavior normally ascribed to the students they teach. This was my chance to escape Bill and Joe. I joined the women for a shot of tequila, and then, following a couple of shrieks of laughter from the crew at the bar, I left the party, much to their dismay.

It was dark when I returned to the school. I parked on a side street and walked to the rear entrance, disarmed the door, and followed along the dark corridor toward my office. Since my key also opened Joe's office, I slipped in and scanned his school phone log. There were numerous calls to and from 308-269-6996, the number on the card that Maria had left.

Suddenly I heard footsteps in the hallway, and then the clanking sounds of hollow metal. I left Joe's office and peered around the corner. At the far end of the hallway was a man opening the padlock on a locker. He then placed a package inside, re-locked it, and quickly moved away toward the front of the building.

I waited a few minutes before I followed down the dark hallway to the area where the man had been. With hundreds of lockers in that area, it was impossible to know which was the one that had been opened. As I was writing down numbers in that general area, I suddenly felt the presence of someone behind me. I turned to face a frightening image in the dim lighting of that hollow hallway. A small, hunched figure, leaning grotesquely to one side was staring up at me with crossed eyes, breathing heavily. As it turned I saw the deformed ear hole.

June Maris was now pointing a crooked finger at one of the lockers. "This one!" she said in an oddly child-like voice that was barely louder than her breathing.

I thanked her warmly as I wrote down the number. Before leaving, I returned to my office and discovered the locker belonged to Maria Salvador.

VI

I drove straight south along highway 62, then turned west to the trailer park where Maria lived. It was after ten when I got there. Maria was still up, watching TV while three little ones were wrapped in blankets, asleep on the couch.

Taken aback by my surprise visit, she was defensive at first. "These are my nieces and nephews. They are visiting from Mexico. I can show you papers."

After assuring her that I was not here because of the children, I explained what happened at the school that night, and she seemed not surprised, as if she had expected something like this. I urged her to stay away from school until further notice. It would be best if she could find someplace to hide out for a few days. She stood there, looking at the sleeping children for a few moments as if she might never see them again. "I will call Juan tomorrow. He will figure something out."

As I was leaving, Maria's mother came out from one of the bedrooms, looking very worried.

"¿Qué pasó?"

"Nada, Mama. Señor James es de la escuela. Él me trajo libros. ¿Cómo está papá?

"No está bien," the woman replied, looking now at me. "Él necesita ver a un doctor."

I assured them that I would find a doctor for Mr. Salvador on Monday.

On Friday morning at 10:00 the alarm went off, and the school went into lock down mode. Students remained in the classrooms, crouching on the floor while the drug canines sniffed the hallways and the lockers. The search lasted less than an hour, after which classes resumed as normal.

Later, after school let out, Principal Davis came to my office to inform me that drugs had been found in Maria's locker, and that the police would be looking for her. It struck me as strange; this was the first time he visited me since I came to the school. He left as abruptly as he had entered. Shortly after, Joe Sanchez entered his office and closed the door. I waited in the corridor until I was sure no one was around and pressed my ear to the door.

"God damn it, man. I told you, you were getting too close to it. Now she's really gone off the edge. You gotta do something, man. Where's the sister now? OK…You figure it out…Yeah, Yeah… If it's got to be *Geronimo*, then just do it. Get it over with."

What did Sanchez mean by "Geronimo?" I wondered. What kind of trouble had Maria gotten herself into? And who was Sanchez talking to? Then I heard footsteps approaching rapidly from down the hall. I got back to my office just as Miss Leslie rounded the corner. She wanted to speak with me in private.

VII

"It's about Maria," she said, seeming apprehensive, perhaps embarrassed from last night at the bar. "I don't believe those were hers. Not for a second. And I'm afraid she is in some kind of trouble."

I asked about Alana, Maria's older sister.

"When she was a senior, she met a guy from Albuquerque named Bob Lamb. He was here managing a construction project by the river. He was older, in his thirties, but she'd turned eighteen that year, so there was nothing illegal about their affair. It wasn't until later that she learned he was married. As soon as he finished the building project, he was gone. Broke her heart. Then she started using drugs, getting stuff from some of the locals who had worked for Lamb. Rumor had it that she got pretty deep in debt."

I asked if she knew the name of the building project that Lamb had managed in Taos.

"It's called the Rio Connection—a definite boys' club. It's illegal to ban women from going to these kinds of places, but I hear they have ways of making girls feel real uncomfortable…that is, unless they work there."

She paused. "And about last night," she looked down, then toward the window before facing me. "I'm not usually so forward."

I assured Miss Leslie that I enjoyed myself last night, and, more importantly right now, that I also was concerned about Maria and would help in any way I could.

It was six that evening when I arrived at the Sandoval home, where Senora Sanchez informed me that Maria had gone to her brother's house.

Juan lived two miles away on a dead-end dirt road at the edge of an arroyo. The trailer was dark inside when I arrived, and no one answered the door. Circling to the back I was startled at how steep the gully was, and how close to it the steps to the back door were. Suddenly I heard a faint moaning sound inside. I entered through the kitchen door to find broken glass on the floor. A table and chairs were overturned. Lying on the floor in the living room was Juan, bleeding from a head wound.

"Ferry. Ferry took her," he moaned as I helped him to the couch.

It was near dusk by the time the ambulance and police arrived. As usual, Juan refused to name names. It was clear he did not trust the police.

VIII

The Rio Connection was located just off route 68, about twelve miles southwest of Taos. Covering over a hundred acres along the dangerously high cliffs above the Rio Grande, the resort offered a dozen cabin rentals and nine holes of beginner to intermediate golf. It is fair to say that most who went to the Rio Connection were not avid golfers, but more inclined to partake in other activities offered in the Rio Bar and Grill, where there were other games to play—darts, pool, video games, and quickdraw screens.

As I arrived at the resort, the last few golf carts were returning from the darkening fairways, the hat-shaded faces of the golfers partially revealed in the yellow lights of the putting terrace and cart lots. Some of them now took the walkway in front of the main building to their cars parked in the lot at the north end. Others opted for the Rio Bar and Grill.

I parked at the far end of the lot, where I disguised myself with a fake beard, golfer's cap, and stuffed jacket. As I entered the bar, I could smell stale beer, as if the keg lines had not been cleaned in a while. There were several booths near the bar for folks who wanted to eat. Pool tables lined the wall at the far end, and the dart boards and video games were placed intermittently.

It seemed odd that the women working there were not just serving drinks, but also playing the games. They all had long, dark hair and were uniformly dressed in tight black shorts and bikini tops. Most of them appeared to be very skilled at pool and darts, showing little mercy to their male challengers, who, for the most part seemed to enjoy themselves in defeat. What was most remarkable, however, was how young they all appeared.

I noticed a vaguely familiar figure enter hastily through the back door into the kitchen. It took a second, but I realized the man with the Tom Selleck moustache and hoodie was really Joe Sanchez. A few minutes later he hurried back outside. I stood by the front door and watched as his car sped down the driveway and on to Highway 68. I decided to have a look around the premises.

Outside, behind the back of the bar, I found a narrow dirt road leading west through a wooded area toward the river cliffs. I followed the path, which was well worn from golf cart tires. I had walked less than a hundred yards when I heard a cart coming down the trail from the bar. I ducked into the woods and watched as a man in a baseball cap and a black-haired young woman passed by, laughing as the cart swerved back and forth along the trail. Another hundred feet ahead, it stopped in front of a small cabin, into which they entered, the man stumbling, the woman trying to hold him steady.

Keeping the cover of the scrub oaks, I followed the path as it turned north along the river line. I passed four more identical cabins, two of which were dimly lit from within, with carts parked in front. The path then made a left turn—west, toward the very edge of the river cliffs. At the end of the path was another building, this one appearing to be a maintenance shed with no windows and a wide, barn-style door in front, which was padlocked shut. Pressing my ear to the rough wood wall, I could hear the faint, muffled sound of girls speaking in Spanish. And there was the sound of someone moaning.

Circling around the back of the shed, I was startled to see how close it was to the cliff's steep edge. A stairway led down from the back door to a small landing—a 20 feet-long deck that jutted out over the cliff. At the end of the landing was the top of a heavy-duty aluminum ladder. My adrenaline surged as I looked over the edge. The ladder followed the steep angle of the cliff down at least fifty feet to where it was cabled to a small dock of concreted rocks. A whitewater raft was tethered there, rocking nervously against the river's powerful current.

As I stood there at this precipice, the waters roiling below, I heard another golf cart pull up to the front of the shed. Crouching now in the shadows under the back steps, I heard the front barn door slide open, then slam closed.

"Well, now you've really done it, haven't you Maria." From inside the shed, Bill Ferry's voice was cold and deadly. "You know how I hate being lied to. So now we're gonna play rough, just you and me. Can you say *Geronimo?*"

I could barely hear the slurred, sobbing response from Maria, as if she was heavily drugged. Then there was the sound of a brief struggle, followed Ferry's heavy breathing as he dragged her across the floor. He kicked the back door open and was now sliding her down the stairs directly above where I was hiding. Her long black hair streamed behind her head as it knocked against the steps. I could see them both now as he pulled her limp body out across the deck landing.

For the first time since my breakdown three years ago, I wished desperately for a gun in my hand. Ferry was a powerful man, and I knew I was no match for him in a fight. Yet I knew I had to do something.

Ferry was walking backwards down the steps as he pulled Maria out of the shed. I realized suddenly that he would, at some point, have to turn around in order to push her over the edge. I waited until that moment.

As Ferry released Maria and repositioned himself in front of her to face the cliff, I rushed out from under the steps. I tackled him, hurtling us both close to the edge. As we struggled on the landing floor, I managed to land one solid blow to his nose, causing him to bleed profusely. But soon he had the advantage and was on top of me, his bloody hands around my throat. "Fucking Paul James," I heard him pant. "Now it's *Geronimo* for you too."

In that moment of terrible violence, I recall a strange sensation of serenity and acceptance. It seemed that I would not fall down from that precipice.

Instead, I would fly away, floating across the river to a place without pain. And then, just as I was beginning to lose consciousness, I heard a strong voice calling from above. "Bill Ferry, release Mr. James immediately! You are under arrest."

Standing atop the steps of the landing was Principal Jack Davis. At his side were two men in emerald green uniforms.

Bill Ferry, in his desperation to escape, was already climbing down the ladder toward the raft. He was nearly half-way there when the fresh blood on his hands caused him to lose his grip. He plunged in freefall, then hit the concrete dock with a sickening thud. The sound of his death was muted by the rushing waters, and his body was now splayed among the rocks.

IX

Three Mexican teenage girls were found locked in the shed, unharmed, at least physically speaking. Joe Sanchez was apprehended near the Mexican border just before dawn. During the subsequent court hearings, more than twenty accomplices in Bill Ferry's human trafficking ring were tried and convicted to maximum sentences. It was revealed that Ferry had used his whitewater rafting business as a means of transportation—the girls were moved at night to different stations along the river between Taos and Albuquerque.

Both Maria and her brother Juan survived the brutality of Bill Ferry. Maria's sister Alana was found months later on the streets in Albuquerque, much of her life already surrendered to opioid addiction. Yet there was some hope for her. There must always be hope.

The following week, Principal Davis called me to his office. "Mr. James, I believe you did your best as a counselor here. But I'm not so sure that this is your calling in life. Don't you have more important missions than dealing with kids at some little high school in the middle of nowhere?"

I assured him that I did not, and that I would like to stay on here at Geronimo for a while if he would have me.

On the last day of school, I was approached by Linda Leslie, who handed me an envelope, then quickly departed.

Inside the envelope was a beautiful hand painted card from Maria. There was a picture of a golden eagle flying alongside an American bald eagle. Beneath them was a broken-down wall that lay scattered in pieces among green cacti across the desert sand. Arching over both sides was a beautiful rainbow.

Thank you, Mr. James. I wanted you to know how much my whole family appreciates what you did for us. My parents are throwing a party for me tomorrow after the graduation ceremony, and of course you are invited. I hope you can handle hot peppers!

> *Sincerely,*
> *Maria*

P.S. I also invited Miss Leslie. Perhaps you could give her a ride. But I warn you—she is also a very hot pepper!